ASHTA

Radha Viswanath was born in Andhra Pradesh and spent most of her life in Delhi. Trained as a teacher, Radha entered journalism late in life. After a distinguished career as a political correspondent spanning three decades, she retired from active journalism. She has the honour of being the first woman journalist to be admitted in the long and distinguished category of parliamentary journalists, in 2006.

An avid reader with a keen interest in Hindu mythology, she aims to bring the complexities of the Indian political discourse into intricate and rich mythological narratives.

ASHTAMAHISHI
The Eight Wives of Krishna

Radha Viswanath

RUPA

Published by
Rupa Publications India Pvt. Ltd 2018
7/16, Ansari Road, Daryaganj
New Delhi 110002

Sales centres:
Allahabad Bengaluru Chennai
Hyderabad Jaipur Kathmandu
Kolkata Mumbai

ISBN: 978-93-5304-611-8

First impression 2018

10 9 8 7 6 5 4 3 2 1

The moral right of the author has been asserted.

Printed by Thomson Press India Ltd., Faridabad

Introduction

Krishna lived in turbulent times. Political strife was at a peak. Magadha Mahajanapada (kingdom) had formed a Samakhya (confederation) of kingdoms with Karusha, Chedi, Vidarbha, Kalayavana, Pundra, Pragjyotishpura and several other minor janapadas, and used this combined force to expand its area of influence. Different sects of the Yadava clan, which ruled in several minor janapadas, fled in all directions to escape the marauding armies of Magadha Confederation.

In the uncertain political situation in the whole of Aryavarta and other parts of Bharata Khanda, morality and justice were largely compromised. Daughters of royal families came to be used as pawns to curry political favours or achieve political objectives. Krishna opposed this trend vehemently and worked to re-establish dharma. He firmly believed that he was born for this purpose and made it his business to ensure that such practices were stopped. He insisted that a couple should enter matrimony solely on the basis of mutual love and respect.

Krishna married eight women and this principle remained the cornerstone in each and every case. These women contributed to making Krishna what he was. While their names figure in the text of the great epic Mahabharata, nothing much is said about what they were like. Even the Bhagavata, which deals with Krishna, the *sampurna avatar*, does not do justice to these women in Krishna's life.

This work is an attempt to understand the eight women who married Krishna and came to be clubbed together as his *Ashtamahishi* or *Ashtabharya*.

A lithe, young boy, barely out of his teens, sprinted across a courtyard, largely unoccupied at this late evening hour. His dhoti billowed behind him and his thick, long, curly locks bobbed rhythmically at his shoulders. The youth paused briefly outside a hut with a thoughtful look on his face. Krishna's curiosity was piqued!

He hardly ever had formal visitors at home. And he had no clue as to the identity of this stranger who wanted to see him. Agnidyotana. That was the name of the visitor who came for him. But the name, brought to him by a messenger, failed to ring a bell of familiarity, let alone recognition. 'Why does this Agnidyotana want to see me? Who is he? Where has he come from? Does this mean trouble?' he wondered as he peeped inside to get a look at his caller.

He breathed easy when he saw an elderly brahmin standing in the middle of the room. His short dhoti, dusty feet and sweaty body indicated that he had come a long distance. The slight crease of perplexity on Krishna's brow cleared as he recalled seeing him in Kundinapura, when he had called on Rajapita Kaisika of Vidarbha.

Agnidyotana looked at Krishna intently for just a fraction of a moment, his keen eye taking in the *murali* stuck in the youth's yellow silk dhoti, and the peacock feather adorning a headband that held down his lustrous hair. A fleeting look of approval crossed his eyes before he lowered his eyelids.

'I love you; I have committed myself to you from the very moment I first set eyes on you. I am yours not only for this life but for all future lives as well. *Purushottama*, please, oh please, come and take me away…'

Krishna could not suppress a smile. He once again glanced at the brahmin who continued to speak with his eyes closed, as if he was reciting a holy hymn in praise of God Almighty. Krishna also closed his eyes and concentrated on the meaning of the words being said to him. This simple act changed it all. The monotone used by the brahmin was replaced by the deeply emotional voice of a young girl pouring her heart out to her lover.

Agnidyotana had travelled from Kundinapura bearing a message of eternal love from the princess of Vidarbha. Now Krishna saw Rajkumari Rukmini's lovelorn face before him along with the voice he heard. His heart missed a beat and he almost reached out to touch her.

'Since the first moment I set eyes on you seven years ago, I have considered myself your wife, *Yadukulabhushana*. I am sure every girl also wants you as her swami because you are handsome, generous, brave, kind and everything else that a girl desires in her husband…'

Krishna knew that he had to help her. They had never met or spoken to each other, and yet, he was always aware of her presence, even in crowded places. She was amongst the women who served food to him when he went for *bhiksha* as was expected of the brahmachari disciples of Sandipani Acharya. He came to recognize her by her feet and tinkling anklets as she passed by him with serving bowls in hand.

'Dhirodatta! Vasudeva! I have vowed that you will be my husband. I cannot live without your love. If this is denied to me,

I shall certainly die. I cannot go through the *swayamvara* that my brother has arranged for me on the instructions of Magadha's mighty ruler Jarasandha. Please take me away! I know it is impossible while I am at the royal palace, but I shall wait for you at the Mata Parvati temple on the outskirts of the city before the swayamvara. Please come there and take me away, *Praneshwara.'*

Agnidyotana completed rendering his message, but Krishna stayed as he was, with eyes shut and arms crossed across his chest, lost in his own inner world. His mind recalled an earlier occasion when Rukmini had sought his help. It was her swayamvara under similar circumstances. The messenger then was his friend Acharya Swetaketu. Krishna had been unable to respond then.

This time, it was different. There was greater depth and sincerity in Rukmini's message brought by Agnidyotana. He could not let her down a second time. He had to help her. No, that was not true. Preventing Rukmini's proposed marriage to Shishupala was necessary to help himself. He loved Rukmini and his life would be crippled if she did not become his *ardhangini.* He must marry her to save himself from ruin.

Acknowledging this truth helped Krishna make his decision. 'Acharya, I will do my best to comply with the Rajkumari's wishes. I will start from here at daybreak tomorrow. Since you are fatigued after this long journey, I request that you rest here tonight and join me in my chariot for your return to Kundinapura.'

ॐ

'Pitamaha!'

The reverence integral to the word was nowhere in the tone of the voice that uttered it. In fact, it sounded more like 'Pitamaa' rather than 'Pitamaha'—the 'grand' (*maha*) of 'grandfather' turning into 'maa'—'mother'.

'Pitamaa!' Rukmini called again as she burst into Kaisika's bed chambers.

That her grandfather continued with his game of *paccheesi* and did not even look up infuriated her so much that she pushed the paccheesi board off the table and plonked herself by his side on his settee. Her long veil, an important part of royal women's attire, fell over her face, and she pulled it off in a huff, flinging it to the ground in annoyance. None of this elicited a response from her grandfather. He crossed his arms across his chest and leaned back, looking at his petulant grandchild.

'How can you play paccheesi when I am dying with tension?' she complained.

'This is an activity that keeps the mind occupied and keeps worry at bay. You should try it too. It will soothe your nerves,' Kaisika said, putting an affectionate arm around Rukmini's shoulders and kissing the top of her head. He rocked her like a baby and spoke soothingly. 'Do I not know what you are agonizing about? Do you think that the same thoughts are not tormenting me? It is a question of life

and death for you, and your life is a thousand times more precious
to me than my own life,' he murmured into her ears.

Rukmini and her grandfather shared a very special bond. It was
not for nothing that Rukmini called him 'Pitamaa'. He had been
like a mother to her ever since her own mother expired when she
was only a child. She was completely at home in Kaisika's private
chambers and continued to behave like a spoilt child with him.
She would rush to him with all her joys and sorrows, thrills and
trials, complaints about her father, brother or *vadhunika*, constant
accounts of what she did and her justifications for them. Thus was
Kaisika privy to her feelings for Krishna. She would discuss her
love with Kaisika as she would have done with her own mother
or a dear friend.

'Do you think he…'

Kaisika silenced Rukmini with a finger on her lips. 'No, little
one! There is no point now in second guessing whether Agnidyotana
was the right choice as emissary; whether he has the physical
stamina to complete the journey in time or whether he has the
ability to persuade Krishna to do your bidding,' Kaisika continued
to speak into her ear, holding her to his chest and rocking her back
and forth as if he was trying to put a baby to sleep. 'Agnidyotana
is a trusted aide of Acharya Swetaketu, and trust was our primary
requirement. How he conducts himself with Krishna is not in our
hands; we have to rely on his judgement.'

Rukmini sat up and faced her grandfather. Her agitation had
subsided, but her worry persisted. 'Do you think he can make
Krishna come… Acharya Swetaketu, who is his friend, could not…'
her voice trembled with unshed tears and trailed off. 'I went to
see Pitashree; I wanted to tell him to call off the swayamvara even
now; that I don't want to marry that power-hungry Yuvaraja. But
Bhrata Rukmi was there. He is the real villain; he is the one who

wants to get rid of me, so that he can get a new wife for himself.'
Rukmini jumped up in impotent rage.

'Come and sit by me, *Nanhi*—Kaisika used the term of
endearment for a small girl—listen carefully to some advice from
this old man,' Kaisika held out his hand.

'The swayamvara is tomorrow; less than 24 hours away,'
Rukmini muttered by way of explanation, but took her grandfather's
extended hand and sat by him.

'Have faith in your love! The strength of your faith is what will
bring Krishna to you, not Agnidyotana's capabilities.

'Nanhi, I will tell you my own experience. I have not shared
this with anyone till now,' Kaisika paused, gathering his thoughts.
Rukmini's heart went out to the old man who had seen so many
ups and downs in his life. She forgot her own concerns and focused
on her grandfather's words. 'You were a baby and your mother was
very ill. That was the time when Jarasandha attacked Vidarbha. Our
forces were unable to withstand his might, and we lost. I had failed.
Failed as a king and leader of the *janapada*. Your father Bhishmaka
was all that a dutiful son should be and shouldered the unsavoury
and humiliating task of peace negotiations with Jarasandha.

'I had all but given up on life. I was so dejected that I could not
eat or sleep... I just could not accept my defeat. Another calamity
struck us; your mother expired. Bhishmaka placed you in my arms
and set out to rebuild Vidarbha. Rukmi, despite his young age,
stood by his father.

'And you gave me a new purpose in life. Bhishmaka feels
thankful that I was there to take care of you. But the truth is, you
took care of me. Even as a baby who could hardly speak, you took
care of me like a mother. You would not eat anything without
sharing it with me. You showered so much love on me.

'So, my dear, while you are worrying whether Agnidyotana

can bring Krishna to you before your swayamvara tomorrow, I am battling with another concern. I know that Krishna will come for you, and that you will go away with him; make a new life with him. And then...,' Kaisika paused, took a deep breath and lowered his eyes. 'And then...,' his voiced trailed. He could not complete his sentence.

Rukmini hugged him hard. There was no need for words between them. Tears rolled down their cheeks.

They lost track of time. They returned to the present only when they heard the sound of someone clearing his throat and looked up.

Agnidyotana stood there, beaming!

'You will need me!'

That was Balarama, already seated in the chariot before Krishna reached it. Agnidyotana stood by the chariot, not knowing what to do. Krishna signaled to him to climb in and jumped in himself. That was cue enough for the horses to set off.

It was still dark and one could barely make out the silhouette of people in the chariot. For Krishna, the defining feature was his favourite peacock feathers tucked into his headband—something he had not forgotten even on this early morning journey. For Agnidyotana, it was his clean-shaven head with a tuft of hair on top, tied into a tight knot. Balarama could be identified by his height. The elder son of Vasudeva was a head and shoulders taller than Krishna. His voice matched his frame and even when he spoke in a whisper, he frightened sleeping birds. The air was cool and misty. The horses were good and had picked up a nice galloping speed in the as yet deserted streets. Krishna calculated that they would be able to complete the journey by dusk.

'Tell me, what is your plan?' Balarama asked, looking Krishna straight in the eye.

'I will marry Rukmini.' Krishna returned the steady gaze.

'Why?'

'I love her. She loves me.'

'Sure! Bhishmaka Rajendra will happily give away his daughter to you, and Jarasandha and the other kings camping in Kundinapura will bless you with *akshata*,' Balarama's voice was dripping sarcasm.

'No, *Bhaiya*! Rukmini has it all planned. She is required to perform *puja* at the Mata Parvati temple in the outskirts of the city before entering the swayamvara pandal. I will be there at the temple when she comes out after her puja and bring her to Dwaraka with me,' Krishna explained.

'Surely you know that she would have guards with her,' Balarama exclaimed, and then continued, in a softer tone, 'Kanha, it is not merely King Bhishmaka and his son Rukmi who will come after you to protect their family's honour. There is a swayamvara scheduled today and the kings of every janapada we know are in the city. Magadha Samrat Jarasandha will be there! You are inviting a full scale war. Is this really necessary?'

'Of course it is, Bhaiya!' Krishna responded spiritedly. 'This swayamvara is a sham! Like many swayamvaras have become these days. While its stated purpose is to enable the bride to select her husband, that freedom is denied to her. Her parents or brothers make the choice and she is forced to abide by it. Should we not stand up against the practice that facilitates the forging of political alliances in the garb of marriages? Should we allow royal families to barter away their daughters for ulterior motives? Don't our princesses deserve better from life?'

Balarama nodded in agreement thoughtfully. 'I would have expected Jarasandha to have learnt his lesson after what happened at Gomantaka Giri. We spared his life.' He paused, distracted by the fidgeting of Agnidyotana sitting opposite him and asked, 'Acharya, what is bothering you?'

'I…I…I had heard that Krishna had worked a miracle at Gomantaka Giri. That he created a tsunami in the ocean…'

Balarama waved a hand suggestively at Krishna, and the younger brother responded with a smile. 'It was no miracle, Agnidyotana. Magadha Samrat Jarasandha had followed us to Gomantaka Giri when he was informed that we had left Mathura to escape him. He was unable to reach us on the mountain top because the mountain was very steep. Jarasandha set fire around the mountain thinking that we would either burn to death or be forced to come down and be killed by his men.'

'He wants to know how we escaped; how the fire was put out and how and why the waves rose so high,' Balarama prodded, receiving a grateful smile from Agnidyotana for it.

Krishna remained in a meditative mood, his eyes closed. 'It was against dharma. No one can cause so much destruction to nature; annihilate an entire race just to kill two brothers—that too for no good reason. That is what I communicated to the ocean. Would the sea be a mute witness to such wanton destruction, I asked. The ocean responded. It was not a miracle.'

'May I ask a question?' Agnidyotana spoke hesitantly, looking from one brother to the other. 'Why does Jarasandha Chakravarti hate you so much?'

Balarama warmed to the subject. 'Good question, Agnidyotana, a very good question. Why does this mighty ruler want two young Yadava boys dead? Because his *Jameya* (nephew), the all-powerful Kamsa, King of Mathura, died at Krishna's hands.

'Did you know how cruel this Kamsa was, Acharya? How undharmic? He imprisoned his own father, King Ugrasena, to become the king of Mathura. Then, on the basis of a prophecy by some formless voice that said Kamsa would die at the hands of the eighth son born to his sister, he put his newly-wed sister and her husband behind bars so that he could kill their children as soon as they were born. He killed six of their sons, but the next two escaped. Those two are sitting here in this chariot with you.'

'I know sir! I have heard that the *asharirávani*'s prophecy came true. I did not have the good fortune to witness that momentous event, which is celebrated even now by the Yadavas,' Agnidyotana said, nodding happily at Krishna.

Balarama hardly noticed the interruption. He continued with gusto, 'Kamsa deserved to die. He plotted to have Kanha here, killed. He had a rogue elephant let loose on him, and engineered a wrestling match for Krishna with two of the best wrestlers in the land. What a fight! Those two wrestlers—Mushtika and Chanura—were huge, like mountains. On the face of it, Krishna was no match to either of them. But one blow from my little brother, and they collapsed. They bled from their ears, noses and mouths and died right there.'

'How did you manage this feat, Krishna Vaasudeva?' Agnidyotana asked.

'Yes, Kanha, I also want to know. Were you not scared at the sight of those famed wrestlers? And you were but a young boy, barely fifteen years old at that time,' Balarama said.

'No, Bhaiya! I was not scared. I do not let fear colour my thinking. I approach a situation with conviction. I tell myself that dharma will prevail and do what I am called upon to do. I do not think about the consequences.'

'But is it not rash action, if you undertake impossible tasks without proper assessment about possible consequences?' the Acharya questioned.

Krishna looked straight into Agnidyotana's eyes. 'No. Apprehensions about outcomes of actions can only be debilitating. I approach each situation with full conviction,' he said.

Agnidyotana seemed satisfied with this reply. He turned his attention to Balarama, shaking his head slightly. 'The death of Kamsa alone does not seem reason enough for this. Why does the

Magadha Samrat have such intense hatred for you? There must be a stronger reason; a reason so strong that he first attempts to have you brothers eliminated, and when those attempts fail, tries this circuitous route to neutralize you. He cannot be in competition with you—you are not anywhere near his age group; neither are you in the league of kings, nor have you challenged his authority in any manner.'

'You are right, Acharya! What Kanha did is much more than challenging his authority. It is the challenge to his ego, his self-esteem that Jarasandha is unable to accept and cope with.

'At Gomantaka Giri, when we came down after the fires were doused, we were attacked by his confederation's army. We had the Garudas, the natives of Gomantaka Giri, on our side. Jarasandha's men fell like flies and I nearly killed him. I had disarmed him and was about to deal one last fatal blow on his head when Kanha stopped me. Jarasandha is a proud Kshatriya for whom honour is more important than life. Because of Krishna, his life was spared, but his honour was lost. He feels compelled to avenge that,' Balarama said and looked at Krishna.

Krishna had his eyes closed, the palms of his hands resting lightly on his knees. He had a look of intense concentration on his face.

❦

4

The calm of midnight, with just the sound of waves softly breaking ground was a completely new experience for Rukmini, who had lived all her life in the confines of a palace. She gazed into the distance, acutely aware of Krishna by her side.

'Rukmini,' Krishna murmured into her ear, twining his fingers with hers. Rukmini tingled all over. Krishna's touch and his breath as he whispered her name mesmerized her. She wanted to respond, but no sound came out of her lips.

Oh! The moon had never looked more beautiful! How the moonlight shimmered on the constantly advancing waves! It looked as if all the stars in the sky had descended to dance...dance with her in this moment of utmost happiness and contentment.

'Happy?'

'Very.' Even she could not hear her voice. But she knew that Krishna had heard, for he chuckled.

'Do you know why?' Krishna murmured the question into her ear and proceeded to answer it himself. 'Because this is a stolen moment; a forbidden pleasure!' He chuckled again.

'You must know the taste of stolen things better, the habitual thief that you are!' Rukmini mocked him, her shyness suddenly vanishing into thin air. Both of them laughed.

She was alone with Krishna for the first time since that eventful day when she had climbed into Krishna's chariot outside the Mata Parvati temple in Kundinapura. While she was welcomed by Krishna's mother Devaki, sister Subhadra and Balarama's wife Revati, she was quickly separated from Krishna and placed in Devaki's custody. She was told that she could not meet or talk to Krishna till they were formally married at an auspicious *muhurta*, to be decided by Garga Acharya, the Kulaguru of the Yadavas.

Krishna had managed to rouse her after Devaki fell asleep and brought her for a walk along the seashore.

'Praneshwara! Can I ask you something?'

'Why did you not bring me away the last time itself? You came and stopped the swayamvara but returned without even finding out how I felt … felt about you and about the swayamvara …' Rukmini's voice trailed off.

Krishna's voice was serious when he spoke. 'At that time, I had not come to pick a wife for myself, but to exert myself to the best of my abilities to see that dharma prevailed. I, a mere cowherd, had no locus standi to participate in a princess's swayamvara. But as someone whose mission in life is the re-establishment of dharma in the land, I had to intervene when something is done against dharma by the very people responsible for upholding it. I did that, and I was gratified when your father, King Bhishmaka, graciously cancelled the swayamvara.'

'Did it not matter that I have sworn to be your wife for this life and all others after it… That I was friendless in the royal palace… I felt like a trapped bird, who would be handed over in a gilded cage to someone chosen by the strongest king in the region… Someone who is interested only in having Vidarbha in his kitty? Or is it that you also do not care for my love…?' Rukmini's voice was tearful.

Krishna put his other hand over Rukmini's hand protectively. 'Of course I knew…I cared. I knew that you had romantic feelings for me since the first time you saw me in the wrestling ring in Mathura.'

'You are wrong about this, my all-knowing *Prananath*,' Rukmini laughed teasingly. 'I first saw you on the streets of Mathura. You were with Jeshtha Bhrata Balarama and I was with my Vadhunika Suvrata. You were being mobbed by people because you had magically straightened the hunch-backed Trivakra. The two of us were in a chariot, and my brother Rukmi was on horseback. He was hitting people with his whip to make way for us. Jeshtha Bhrata snatched the whip and my brother fell off. The bullocks of our rath panicked and we would have fallen off too, if you had not pacified the bullocks... I fell in love with you that very moment. That was seven years ago...'

They sat in silence, each thinking of the time when Kamsa had organized week-long festivities on the eve of his *dhanushyagna*. For Krishna and Balarama, it was their first-ever visit to this magnificent city. It was Rukmini's first visit to Mathura as well. Her brother Rukmi and Kamsa were good friends and close followers of Jarasandha, the King of Magadha. Rukmini knew that Krishna would be there and wanted to ascertain that the songs and stories she heard from wandering groups of minstrels were indeed true, that Krishna was a miracle worker.

'Who is Radha?' Rukmini surprised herself with the question and bit down hard on her tongue. She could give the world to withdraw the words.

Krishna laughed. He let go of her hand and turned to face her. 'I was expecting this and must confess that I am surprised that you took so long to ask.'

'I am sorry... Please pardon me, Purushottama, please trust me, it was not my intention to pry into your past. I am happy, I am honoured that you accepted my love. There is nothing more that I desire in this life.' Rukmini was contrite, wringing the edge of her *pallu*.

'No, *Priye*! You should not enter matrimony with any doubt. Matrimony is the most sacred of bonds and the partners must have full faith in each other. So, stop worrying and listen. I will tell you everything about her.

'Radha lost her mother when she was very young, merely a toddler. Her stepmother was unwilling to raise her. So she was taken in by her grandmother. The grandmother expired in due course and she returned to her father in Vrindavan. I was about seven years old when she came to visit her relatives in Gokul. I had fallen and had bruised myself. Radha washed my wounds and her touch felt divine and soothing. She was twelve or thirteen—some five or six years older than I was. We became great friends and she was sad when it was time for her to go back.

'As it happened, we all had to leave Gokul to protect our cattle from hyenas. The entire village relocated to Vrindavan and all of us—Bhaiya, Uddhava, the other boys and girls from Gokul—were happy to revive our friendship with Radha. We played, sang and danced on the beautiful banks of the Yamuna. On moonlit nights, there used to be long hours of *raas*. All the *gopikas*, or maidens, participated with gusto, but Radha's stepmother did not approve of the 19-year-old Radha playing with boys. She would punish Radha—lock her up in a room, beat and starve her. She was worried that Radha's marriage, arranged with a soldier in Kamsa's army, would fall through if the groom's side learned of her wayward ways.

'Her fears came true. The marriage was cancelled by the boy's parents and Radha was thrown out by her stepmother.'

'Where is she now? How terrible to become orphaned like that!' Rukmini's heart melted for this unfortunate girl.

'How is she an orphan, when I am there! She loves me. She

constantly thinks of me. I cannot but reciprocate such devotion and commitment. Radha is in Vrindavan, in my mother Yashoda's care.' Krishna's voice had a huskiness and dreaminess to it.

'Do you miss her?' She could not help the question.

'No. Where is the question of missing her? She is the music that comes from my murali. She inspires me. She is a part of me at all times!'

It was as if Krishna had revealed his soul to Rukmini. She felt she had merged with her husband-to-be—soul to soul, spirit to spirit. She was not even surprised at her unusual reaction to the situation. There was peace within her, peace around them.

A stern voice broke the spell. It was Balarama who had come looking for them. 'I knew Krishna would do something like this. What good is growing up, if he cannot stop his naughty tricks!' he said as he pulled his younger brother up.

Rukmini, whose cheeks had grown beetroot pink in mortification at having been caught by Balarama, walked a couple of steps behind the two brothers. They were very different physically. Balarama was very tall and muscular. Krishna was of medium build, barely touching his elder brother's shoulders. Balarama was fair—so fair as to be visible in pitch darkness. Krishna was the opposite. He was dark as the darkest cloud. Yet, they loved each other unconditionally.

Rukmini's lips parted in a smile as she recalled the way the two brothers, Krishna particularly, cuddled up to their mother. Krishna was like a little child who hadn't seen his mother for long. Rukmini remembered the first time she saw the mother-son duo hug each other. It was when Krishna returned home after slaying a rogue elephant, wrestlers Chanura and Mushtika and Mathura King Kamsa. The extremely distraught Devaki stretched out her arms and Krishna had snuggled into the folds of her saree. No one would have believed it was the same young lad who had just dealt out four deaths! Rukmini had realized that Krishna was responding to his mother's concern. She fell in love with him all over again for this quality.

Her thoughts drifted to her own mother. She never knew her, having lost her soon after birth. She grew up amidst three men—a doting Pitamaha, an equally loving Pitashree and a rather strict Bhrata. The only female family member she knew was her vadhunika, Suvrata. Their relationship had failed to gain depth. Life had undergone a qualitative change after Pitamaha Kaisika lost the war with Jarasandha of Magadha. Kaisika immediately renounced the throne and went into retirement. Bhishmaka succeeded him as king and made peace with Jarasandha, but somehow, Pitashree was a broken man. He became very submissive and brother Rukmi emerged as the de facto ruler of Vidarbha.

Rukmini's pace had slackened. Krishna and Balarama were way ahead and she could barely make out their forms in the distance. She suddenly stiffened; the nape of her neck tingled. She knew the feeling; she was being followed!

Who could it be! Who was interested in having her spied upon in Mathura? Was it some local leader jealous of Krishna? Or her brother Rukmi, to avenge his humiliation for having failed to prevent her abduction? Or could it be someone deputed by Jarasandha and Sisupala?

She quickened her pace. She did not want any trouble just three days before her wedding.

Rukmini heaved a sigh of relief when she realized that whosoever was following her, knew that she was aware of their presence and sidled away in the darkness.

☙

'Maaaa…'

Satyabhama's anguished cries, which wracked her body, were lost into the softness of a pillow that she clutched to her bosom, and buried her face in. It was already drenched with her tears.

Her life was over! She had nothing to live for!

Satya looked wildly around her room. It dripped opulence. It was elegant. But what use were all these when she did not have a single friend to share them with! She did not even have a mother to comfort, advise and guide her. She felt lonely and forsaken.

She was heartbroken ever since her messengers—she did not like to call them spies—informed her that Krishna had been walking hand-in-hand with the girl he had abducted. The couple seemed very happy and turned homeward only when Balarama arrived and chided them. This confirmed her worst fears—Krishna was in love with Rukmini. How can a *gopala*, with a free spirit typical of people who spend their days under the open sky, fall for a princess, whose life was cloistered in a palace? And what does royalty know about love? Royalty, after all, is only primness and protocol!

And she, Satya, had loved Krishna for as long as she could remember, maybe from the very first moment when she had set eyes on him. She remembered that short trip to Gokul. She was just over five years of age and her father Satrajit had taken her to watch the annual Indrotsava. This was a festival that all Yadavas celebrated as a community event to propitiate Indra, the God of rain. Krishna, a boy of seven or eight, stood out in the crowd, whether he was playing with other children or was called upon by the priests conducting the *yagna* to fetch and carry. Krishna's smiling face, the peacock feather in his headband and the murali tucked at his waist were memories that remained with Satya ever since. She got to see more of him when her father, a Yadava *mukhya*, shifted to Mathura after Kamsa's death and Ugrasena's reinstatement as king.

Actually, Satyabhama, who saw Krishna after some years since that Indrotsava, initially didn't think much of him. She agreed with her father that he was a fool to have declined the offer of the crown of Mathura. The aging King Ugrasena, who was imprisoned by his son Kamsa in order to become king himself, had said that he was old and incapable of managing the kingdom's affairs. He was also grieving the death of his only son, even as he acknowledged that it had become necessary to save the people from Kamsa's tyranny. Krishna should have accepted the position of King. Instead of grabbing the chance, Krishna pleaded with Ugrasena to resume his position. If he needed help with the administration, the Yadava Mukhyas of various sects would form an advisory council and assist the King in discharging his responsibilities, Krishna had assured.

While Satyabhama was too young to understand the implications of this new arrangement, Krishna had actually converted a monarchy into a system of participative governance. Under the changed rules of governance, agreement among the Mukhyas was necessary and these decisions were binding on the King. The Sabha of Mukhyas could summon any citizen, either for questioning or for consultations. Any citizen could petition the Sabha on any issue. The Mukhyas' Sabha consisted of leaders of all Yadava sects—the Bhojas, Bahukas, Andhakas, Satyakas, Dasarhas,

Vrishnis, Shuras and so on, which ensured that there was no unjust discrimination against anyone in any matter.

Satya decided she would have nothing with Krishna, who did not know to further his own interests. Satrajit, who was nominated to the council of advisors, realized that Krishna, despite not being a member of the Mukhya Sabha, would remain a dominant figure in Mathura's public life. That could be detrimental to the furtherance of his ambition, he thought and started cultivating his own separate group of supporters. He would position himself as an alternate power centre with Brihadbala as its royal face. Brihadbala was Kamsa's *bhagineya* who aspired to ascend the throne after Ugrasena, as Kamsa was childless. Brihadbala, however, lacked leadership qualities to lead a conglomerate of Yadava sects. These sects themselves lacked unity and needed a person of strong character to lead them; Brihadbala was definitely not such a charismatic leader.

Satrajit nursed secret ambitions for the top position and was willing to use his considerable riches to realize his dream. He knew that this would not happen as long as Krishna was in Mathura. He tried to tarnish Krishna's reputation to improve his own standing among the Yadavas. For Satyabhama, the only child of Satrajit, snide comments berating Krishna and plans for his downfall were a regular part of growing up and, for some years, she shared her father's perception of Krishna.

Satya was not aware when her disdain for Krishna had turned into admiration, respect and affection. For a while, she fancied herself as the object of Krishna's attention, given her acknowledged beauty and impressive wealth. That did not happen, but Satya's love only grew as she came to respect Krishna's forthright ways and his unstinting efforts to help others.

A similar transformation did not come about in Satrajit. His animosity towards Krishna only increased with time. He did, however, admit that it was not easy to counter Vaasudeva's popularity. Krishna was often called Vaasudeva, meaning 'son of Vasudeva'. Thinking of Krishna as someone's son helped Satrajit convince himself that he was dealing with a youngster, and so he would succeed sooner or later.

Satrajit was also aware that Yuyudhana, also called Satyaki—son of Satyaka, was slipping from his grasp. Yuyudhana was, in fact, the brightest and most capable to counter Krishna and it was this ambition that encouraged him to join forces with Satrajit. In a bid to retain him on his side, Satrajit offered his daughter Satyabhama in marriage. The proposal failed to make headway because Satyaka was against it and Satyaki himself was not ready for marriage as yet. He wanted to hone his skills in martial arts further and joined Acharya Sandipani's gurukul.

Joining the gurukul proved to be a turning point in Satyaki's life. He came into close contact with Krishna and Balarama, who also were Sandipani Acharya's disciples. He recognized Krishna as a conscientious student who followed the Guru untiringly all through the day and spent his nights discussing philosophical issues, while massaging their teacher's tired legs. Acharya Sandipani was a master in the making of arms, in addition to Vedic knowledge, diplomacy, administration, martial arts and the training and management of animals. Very soon, Satyaki became an admirer and friend of Krishna. His desire for name, fame and power vanished completely and he became an ardent subscriber to Krishna's vision of a world where dharma prevailed.

For Satrajit, however, dharma remained an empty word. He scoffed that Krishna used it to divert attention from his foolhardy escapades; an excuse to justify undue interference in the internal matters of different kingdoms. Why should a Yadava army march for weeks on end to prevent Rajkumari Rukmini's wedding? It was a matter between Rukmini's father, King Bhishmaka of Vidarbha, and Shishupala's father, King Damaghosha of Chedi. 'Dharma,' Satrajit argued, 'was a figment of Krishna's fertile imagination that led to the Yadavas getting involved in every fight anywhere in Aryavarta. Why should the Yadavas expend their blood for others' causes? Instead, if they concentrated on their own lives and affairs, they stood a better chance at progress and would be respected in the local community.'

Satyabhama remembered the time when Krishna had come calling on her father. He had tried to explain the concept of dharma to Satrajit and its significance in human life. Satrajit had his counter arguments ready. The Yadavas were attacked several times by Jarasandha, King of Magadha. 'Did any king from anywhere in Aryavarta come to help us or stand by us?' he asked. 'So, why should we involve ourselves in what they do amongst themselves?'

Satrajit argued forcefully that the Yadavas would, in fact, gain from wars in Aryavarta. 'While they lose their assets and men to war, the Yadavas, by focusing on improving their assets, would emerge stronger and more powerful.'

Krishna either guessed that it was futile to try and convince Satrajit, or did not have arguments to counter these points. He went away without another word.

'But I am not like Krishna,' Satyabhama told herself. 'I do not give up! I persist with my efforts till I get what I want,' she said. She rose from her bed, straightened herself and looked at her reflection in a mirror and twirled the ends of her thick, long and black hair around her fingers. 'I am Satyabhama! I never lose! I never accept defeat! I get what I want!'

'Satya wants Krishna as her husband. So he will be become Satya's husband,' she told her reflection in the mirror. She paced up and down, thinking. She stopped in front of the mirror after a while and in a voice that displayed her determination, said, 'Krishna will not only become Satyabhama's husband, but be known as "Satyabhama's husband". That will be his identity. He will himself say that Satyabhama is better than Rukmini. I will make him say that.'

'Krishna, you will be called "Satya-Pati" soon,' she declared and stepped out with a song on her lips.

6

'Rukkooo!'

The door burst open almost simultaneously, and an excited Krishna rushed in and swept Rukmini off her feet into his arms. He turned her round and round with a musical chant of 'Rukkoo, Rukkoo'—a throwback to his days of *raasleela* in Vrindavan several years ago. He stopped only when he was forced to—both his legs got entangled in a saree that she was folding. Krishna ensured that he collapsed on a nearby settee with Rukmini still in his arms.

'Now that you are done with dancing, my dear Govinda, please tell me what makes you so happy,' Rukmini said, trying to separate her saree from their bodies. Krishna stopped her, shaking his legs impatiently to free them. He cupped her face in both his hands and bringing his face very close to hers whispered, 'Yudhishtira has been nominated Yuvaraj!'

Rukmini tingled all over with excitement. She knew the import of these words. Her communion with her husband was so complete and comprehensive that Rukmini did not need to be told anything at all. Just one look from him and she knew. Similarly, she never needed to say anything much to Krishna. He just had to look at her face to get her response to whatever was troubling him. In fact, that simple act of looking at Rukmini soothed his soul. But often, Rukmini would act as if she needed explanations, just for the satisfaction of seeing him relive his happiness and doubling his happiness through sharing with his wife. She also knew that such sharing also enabled her husband to organize his own thoughts. More than everything else, both immensely enjoyed these conversations.

This time too, Rukmini knew the larger implications of this development in Hastinapura. Yudhishtira, with Bhishma Pitamaha and Vidura Babu guiding him along, would be able to secure Panchala Maharaja Drupada's cooperation to contain the expansionist designs of Jarasandha of Magadha. This was vital for revival of dharma in Aryavarta. At least that was what Krishna believed. After all, friendly relations between Hastinapura and Panchala—the two most powerful kingdoms along the banks of Ganga—would guide the destiny of the entire region.

However, Rukmini decided to play ignorant. That would give her a chance to provoke Krishna. She loved his pout when he was exasperated with her. 'But that was only waiting to happen. He is next in the line of succession!'

'Then you know nothing. Do you even know who Yudhishtira is?' The flick of his right hand and pulling away from Rukmini showed his irritation.

Rukmini's eyes sparkled. 'After being married to you for about two years, I can now say that I know most of your *bandhujan* (relatives). You cannot even imagine what a huge exercise that was— knowing your numerous *Bhavukas*, *Bhratvajas*, *Pitruvyas*, *Pitrushyas* and *Swasuras*,' Rukmini said, trying to hide the chuckle in her voice.

'Remember, I came from a very small family—just Pitamaha, Pitashree and Bhrata. Vadhunika Suvrata was only a distant presence; she was only interested in securing her husband, Bhrata Rukmi's, affection,' she added by way of explanation.

Rukmini's game plan worked. Krishna was quick with his retort. 'Why do you talk as if that is a huge problem? I also started with a small family—Mahee and Bapu (Yashoda and Nanda), *Badi-maa* (Rohini) and Bhaiya Balarama.

'My world overturned when I was turning fourteen. I was translocated from Vrindavan to Mathura; told that Mahee and Bapu were not my "real" parents; that Bhaiya is my blood-brother, not Badi-maa's son,' Krishna paused, reliving the trauma of that experience. Rukmini reached out and placed an understanding hand over his arm.

Krishna patted his wife's hand. 'I need no sympathy, my dear! Just think of Mahee and Bapu! They knew all along that I was not born to them. Yet, showered all their love on me; took all the trouble I piled on them without complaining, and let me go when Pitruvya Akrura came to claim me!'

'Such pure and all-encompassing love!' Krishna mused, slipping into a past that was very dear to him. 'We had very little education in Vrindavan. Garga Acharya would teach us whenever he came over from Mathura. *Jiyya* and *Jijiya*, his biological parents—Vasudeva and Devaki, decided that we had to have intensive learning and training. Sandipani Acharya graciously accepted us as his disciples. We were initiated into brahmacharya, and we followed our guru everywhere,' Krishna paused.

When he spoke again, he was speaking to himself. 'That one single year changed me!'

'One year... And my life, my world, my objectives, my goals... everything changed. I, who only knew to graze cattle, play with gopalas and gopikas, play my murali and enjoy raas with girls who called me "Kanha". That Kanha is lost forever,' he paused, thinking of that carefree phase of his life.

Rukmini waited. When he resumed, his mind had shifted to his days at Sandipani Ashram. 'Sandipani Acharya is highly learned. He is committed to the establishment of dharma in each and every human being. That is why he travelled from place to place, teaching, training and spreading awareness among kings and commoners alike. These travels kept him abreast of developments across Aryavarta.

'He took us along wherever he went. He taught us the four Vedas, *vaidickratu*s or procedures, *rajaneeti* or politics, *sanatana* dharma, warfare and the dharma of warfare, training of horses and elephants for war, martial arts, wrestling and boxing, sword-fights, archery and so on. He also taught us the use of different weapons, their specific advantages and designing and making them. Training under this very talented student of Parasurama has instilled a commitment towards dharma in me. I have to exert myself and ensure that dharma prevails everywhere at all times.'

'And you think this lofty goal is achievable with Yudhishtira as Yuvaraja in Hastinapura,' Rukmini said.

'I feel it takes me closer to my goal—the cherished goal of my life,' Krishna paused. His eyes were half closed. 'Yudhishtira, the eldest of Pandavas, being named Yuvaraja means that Bhishma Pitamaha and Vidura Babu have prevailed on Dhritarashtra, who wanted his son Duryodhana anointed as Yuvaraja. Had that happened, Hastinapura's prestige as a righteous kingdom would have suffered irreparable damage. You see, Duryodhana depends on his Mamaka Shakuni for advice and Shakuni's priorities in life are different and his methods generally not in accordance with dharma.

'I am happy that finally this has been resolved, and it is Yudhishtira, not Duryodhana, who will ascend the throne. I am told that Yudhishtira is shaping up well and is gaining public approbation. Now, my very dear friends Bhima and Arjuna can also come into their own and help their elder brother in administration and bloom to the fullest of their potential.'

'I find it very surprising that the Kauravas and Pandavas, descendants of the same dynasty and children of two brothers brought up and taught by the same set of people, are still so different,' Rukmini mused, more to herself than saying it aloud for a comment from her husband.

'There is also news that my bhavukas Vinda and Anuvinda, sons of Pitrushya Rajadhidevi and Swasura Jayasena, the King and Queen of Avanti, are shaping well and making a name for themselves as good archers. Additionally, Avanti is acquiring a reputation as a centre of learning.'

'I am sure that is great news for the king and queen,' Rukmini said.

'Another good tiding is that Magadha Maharaja Jarasandha has remained confined to Girivraja, his capital and content with managing his kingdom. I hear that he has not taken kindly to the failure of his plans for your marriage to Chedi Yuvaraja Shishupala,' Krishna laughed.

Normally, Rukmini would have responded with a crisp retort to this, but she realized that Krishna had other thoughts to share. She nodded and waited for him to go on.

'You know Vaidarbhi, dharma can be revived in Aryavarta only if Jarasandha is contained. For this to happen, it is necessary that Hastinapura stays strong and persuades Panchala to tread the same path. These two kingdom on the banks of Ganga are the most powerful in the region. They are like the heart of Aryavarta. Now that Yudhishtira is at the helm in Hastinapura, we can convince Drupada Maharaja to see reason.'

Krishna sat up straight. He had made a decision. 'I think I will go to Hastinapura and be with Yudhishtira for a year or so, and help him to advance the cause of dharma.' Krishna was interrupted by the entry of a messenger with news that Sandipani Acharya had come and wanted to see him.

ॐ

Krishna sat staring into the swirling waters of the sea, unheeding of the howling winds and gathering clouds on the horizon, lost in his inner world of contemplation.

Acharya Sandipani's visit had unsettled all his plans and dashed all his hopes. Hastinapura had seen dramatic developments in the recent few weeks. Yudhishtira had not only been dethroned, but exiled, along with all his brothers and mother. The decision, according to the Acharya, was stated to have been taken to avert family feuds between cousins escalating to a full-blown war.

With Yudhishtira no longer in charge in Hastinapura, Krishna's hopes and expectations of forging strong bonds of friendship between the Kuru and Yadava Kingdom and then moving on to involve Panchala in confronting Magadha had collapsed. In the process, his plan to establish dharma had received a body blow. Even more worrying was the information that the Pandavas had been sent to Varanavata, a place in the midst of forests. That the place was specifically selected by Dhritarashtra could only mean danger to the lives of the exiled family.

Another bit of information conveyed by the Acharya, despite being of a very different nature, also threatened his strategy for peace in the region. Drupada, King of Panchala, had invited Krishna to Kampilya, the capital of Panchala, to offer his daughter Draupadi in marriage to Krishna.

Krishna's immediate instinct was to reject the proposal. The proposal had its roots in politics—the long-standing animosity between Drupada and Drona Acharya, teacher of military arts to Kuru Kumaras and overall incharge of Hastinapura's armed forces as *senapati*. He reminded the Gurudev of his personal conviction that marriage should be based solely on love and mutual respect and that there should be no links between politics and personal lives. In this case, Drupada had proposed the alliance not because he thought there would be love between his daughter and Krishna, but to obtain an ally against Dronacharya.

'Consider its repercussions,' Sandipani Acharya had said. 'It is not for nothing that I brought this proposal to you personally. Keep your larger goal in mind while taking your decision,' Gurudev said before leaving.

Krishna had to admit that it was a very complex issue. Drupada aimed at getting his revenge against Dronacharya through his daughter's marriage. While set against any such deals in the name of marriage, Krishna knew that refusing this offer would lead to greater complications and worsen the situation. If he agreed to the marriage, the Yadavas would get drawn into the Drupada–Drona feud. If he refused, Draupadi would be bartered away as a bride to Jarasandha's *poutra* Meghasandhi; Panchala's freedom would stand bartered to Magadha and a whirlpool of hatred and war would engulf the entire region. The Yadavas could not remain isolated from developments in the region—they would be dragged into it, even if they resisted it.

Drupada and Drona were best friends turned worst enemies. Both were born almost at the same time and had identical circumstances of birth. Drupada was born when his father, King Prishata of Panchala, who chanced upon the *apsara*, Menaka, while she emerged from a river after a bath. An aroused Prishata ejaculated, which immediately transformed into a child. In case of Drona, his father, Maharshi Bharadwaja, was tormented by thoughts of Ghritachi, an apsara. While trying to perform a yagna, a sperm fell into a *droni*, or a bowl made of leaf. To his amazement, it turned into a child! While Rishi Bhardwaja was raising his *ayonija*—not born out of a womb—son, whom he named 'Drona' on account of his birth in a *droni*, King Prishata did not want to take his ayonija son back with him. He left him at Bharadwaja's *ashram* and returned to Kampilya.

The two similarly-born boys, Drupada and Drona, grew up together like twins at the ashram. They were inseparable as friends and shared everything. They promised each other that they would remain friends for life, sharing everything equally at all times. This idyllic friendship ended when King Prishata took his son back for coronation as king. A few years later, Drona called on the young king and demanded half of the kingdom in accordance with their agreement at the Bharadwaja ashram. Drupada laughed at his friend for holding him to a childhood promise and offered him a teacher's post in his kingdom. Drona left feeling betrayed and humiliated, and determined to teach him a lesson for not honouring a solemn promise.

Drona undertook rigorous training to master martial arts, trained his own students—the Kauravas and Pandavas of Hastinapura—and demanded the capture of Drupada as *guru-dakshina*. Bhima and Arjuna accomplished the task by ambushing the king while he was on vacation. Drona released his former friend after making him apologize for insulting him and taking away half his kingdom. In the process, the all-consuming fire of revenge kindled within Drupada.

While his Brahmin friend Drona took the Kshatriya path of war to get his revenge, the Kshatriya king Drupada took the Brahminical path of *tapas* to fulfill his own pledge. Years of austerities produced two children—a son, Drishtadyumna, and a daughter, Draupadi. Drupada did not let them ever forget that their main purpose in life was to revenge Drona.

However, Drupada realized that he needed to buttress his strength further to achieve his objective, as Drona was now in a powerful position in Hastinapura and his son Ashwatthama was a trusted friend of crown prince Duryodhana. Marrying his daughter Draupadi to a reputed warrior was the strategy Drupada hit upon to avenge himself. Krishna emerged as the frontrunner among the potential grooms reviewed by the king.

Krishna was confused. What should he do? What was the right thing to do? He could not refuse to marry Draupadi, nor could he agree to it. Either way, the result would only be war and destruction. Was he even right in holding on to dharma? What was dharma? Can humans, with their myriad limitations and desires, be inspired to follow dharma? Have I adhered to dharma at all times? Questions tormented him. He had no answers. He lay back on the sand and closed his eyes.

Krishna opened his eyes when he felt his head being raised. A faint smile appeared on his face as he realized that it was his wife, attempting to cradle his head in her lap. Neither spoke and Krishna felt his cares melt under Rukmini's soft fingers soothing his brow and running through his hair.

'Do you know what your dharma is, Vaidarbhi?'

Krishna felt her smile, even though his eyes were shut. 'My dharma is really small, Nath! I want to live within you so that my heart is a happy dwelling place for you. There is nothing more that I desire beyond being able to support you in every action of yours. That way, I feel I augment your strength.'

'You are my strength, Rukkoo. With you next to me, I feel

I can achieve my goals. All my problems dissolve miraculously.'

Rukmini's fingers pushed back a strand of hair from his brow. She then asked, 'What is dharma?'

'Vaidarbhi! I am also trying to find an answer to this question. It has been tormenting me since my meeting with Gurudeva Sandipani Acharya this evening. At this moment, all I can say is that dharma is not desire; it is not assumptions, rules and regulations. Dharma is not born out of passion, anger or fear. Dharma is that which can train men and circumstances to overcome weaknesses.'

Krishna opened his eyes and looked into the dark depths of Rukmini's eyes. He smiled and said, 'I know what you really want to know—the purpose of Acharya's visit and the dilemma that I am trying to grapple with.' Krishna reached up and cupped her chin.

'The very existence of Aryavarta is now threatened, all because of one small vengeful deed. A foolish king of a very small kingdom insulted a proud Brahmin. This Brahmin dedicated his life to avenging this insult. In the process, he bred anger, hatred and vengeance within himself, forgetting his dharma as a Brahmin. The king retaliated by not only filling himself with thoughts of revenge, but also injecting that poison into his children. The Brahmin has grown into a warrior and the king followed the Vedic route to beget blessed children who can defeat this Brahmin. This personal animosity has made Hastina and Panchala sworn enemies and now, all of us are getting dragged into it.

'I had not realized that hatred could be so powerful and all consuming! For dharma to prevail, we need to keep this negative emotion in check. Otherwise, it will swallow everything else. So, if we expand and apply it on a general scale, we can say that it is necessary to keep hatred and anger under check.

'But...is it wrong to seek revenge?' Rukmini asked diffidently.

Krishna sat up, looking intently into her eyes. He put his arm around her shoulders and answered earnestly, 'No, my dear! It is not at all wrong to seek revenge. In fact, it is every person's right to seek redressal for injustices done to him or her. That is dharma. Those that cannot secure such redressal are considered incapable and weak. However, it is those that have the capacity to be revenged, yet shun such action, and prefer to pardon the perpetrator of the injustice, who are great human beings. These are wise people,' Krishna said as he pulled his wife up by the hand. Both started walking back home, hand in hand.

'Let us examine this very case of Drona and Drupada. Drona is a Brahmin; a learned man. His word carries more power than the deadliest of missiles. But he behaved like a Kshatriya, nurturing hatred to be revenged. He, thus, slipped from his dharma as a Brahmin.'

'Do you mean then that Drona should not have sought vengeance?'

'No! Only that there should have been a purpose to his vengeance! And that should be to wipe out negativity and reform the perpetrator of the unjust act. Here, Drona's action, instead of making Drupada realize his mistake and reform, ended up multiplying the same hatred manifold. This can only unleash an unending saga of revenge. Actions devised to deal with injustices should lead to removal of hatred and replacement with love.'

Rukmini fell into a thoughtful silence. But as she slipped into bed next to him, she put her arm around his neck and whispered, 'Then you should go to Kampilya and talk to the king.' After a moment of silence, she added, 'Marry Draupadi if proves to be necessary.'

ॐ

8

The atmosphere in the Mukhyas' Sabha in Dwaraka was electric. Almost everyone was there, for it was a session requisitioned by Krishna Vaasudeva, son of Mukhya Vasudeva. Any such session convened at the request of Krishna attracted much attention, because Krishna had earned the reputation of coming up with novel propositions that had immense impact on the quality of life of the common man.

Yet, this particular session was different. Unlike in the past, when Krishna's presentations in the Mukhyas' Sabha were awaited with eager anticipation, there was a strong undercurrent of opposition brewing against Krishna. This time round, the predominant emotion among the participants in the Sabha was apprehension. The Yadavas had prospered significantly since relocating to Dwaraka, mainly on account of having access to a sea-route, a rich source of business. Most Yadavas lived in considerable luxury, had accumulated assets and many had even learned to take time off to enjoy their wealth.

King Ugrasena was presiding over the session. All the Mukhyas were seated in their assigned seats to the right of the King's throne. Krishna, who had requisitioned the meeting, occupied a small enclosure to the left of the conference hall, directly facing the Mukhyas. There was another small enclosure next to this one, which was intended for any member of the community who desired to intervene in the debate. There were two sections directly in front of the king's throne to seat the general public, one for men and another for women and children.

Satrajit, sitting in the front row to the right of the throne, looked around with satisfaction. He had invested heavily in building a strong support base for himself. He was determined to push Krishna and his small band of supporters into insignificance and enhance his own importance and reputation among the Mukhyas. His work of several years had come to fruition; he could see from the impressive crowd that had filled the enclosure intended for potential speakers on issues under debate. In contrast, Krishna barely had half-a-dozen men with him, Satyaki being the only known face among them.

'Krishna Vaasudeva, you desired to be heard. Please state your case,' King Ugrasena's words brought the assembly to order. Krishna rose to speak as the muted chatter of the expectant public ceased.

'Maharaja, I sought the meeting of the Sabha to highlight certain important developments in our neighbourhood. There has been an upheaval in Pushkar. Its ruler King Chekitana has been dethroned in an armed aggression by Hastinapura. Pushkar is a very small janapada, and so, naturally, did not have the ability to repel the disproportionately large force that invaded it. King Chekitana had been driven into the jungles. I urge upon this Sabha to sanction remedial action to reinstate Chekitana as king.'

'Maharaja, I seek your indulgence. I have a point to make in this regard.' It was Jayasena, who had jumped up to interrupt Krishna even before he completed speaking.

'Maharaja, I want to know how we are concerned with whatever happened in Pushkar. It is but a tiny little janapada on the banks of Yamuna river. It has little or no political clout in Aryavarta, or even among the Yadava janapadas. Why should we, located so far away, make it our business to interfere?'

The assembly reverberated with shouts of 'yes, why? Tell us

why? How are we concerned with it?' and Ugrasena asked Krishna to answer this question. The Sabha needed to be fully convinced on the need and justification for any action.

'*Prabhu*, I feel that our responses to developments should not be merely on the basis of how they affect us. I agree that the significance of Pushkar does not lie in its size. Yet, there is a locational aspect that makes it important. Pushkar lies close to the highway that connects the various Yadava janapadas. Having a friendly Yadava Mukhya in charge in Pushkar will facilitate transport and communication among the Yadava janapadas and strengthen them all.

'In addition, there is the larger issue of dharma. The aggression against Pushkar was uncalled for and against dharma. Therefore, Raja Chekitana should be helped to undo this undharmic occupation.'

Several members stood up, vociferously opposing Krishna's proposal. Such was the dissent that Raja Ugrasena had difficulty restoring order. This was the first time ever that Krishna faced such opposition in the Sabha. Satrajit rose and held up a hand seeking silence.

'Maharaja, I really do not understand why we go into a frenzied chest-beating mode about adharma. What is dharma and adharma? These are but words that Krishna uses to compel people to do what he wants. Krishna is clever and very persuasive with his words and charm. If Dwaraka is to base all its actions on these two words, it may not be long before we get involved in every fight in Aryavarta. Why should the Yadavas shed blood to redress someone else's perceived injustices?' he asked.

Krishna's eyes widened in surprise when he saw the next person who rose to oppose the proposal. It was his own elder brother Balarama. Krishna lowered his eyes to hide his reaction and concentrated on what was being said. 'Maharaja, it is natural for kings to try and expand the area of their influence. There is no great issue of dharma involved in this. In the case under discussion here, King Duryodhana of Hastinapura was the attacker. King Chekitana of Pushkar, being the weaker of the two, lost. I would think it is dharma that the winner, King Duryodhana, is allowed to retain Pushkar.

'However, I think we must show some consideration to King Chekitana, because he is also a Yadava. Since Raja Chekitana is now rendered homeless, I suggest that we should give him an honorable place to relocate. He may be invited to Dwaraka, where he can settle as a Mukhya.'

When called upon to respond to these submissions, Krishna argued that Dwaraka could not be blind to developments in the neighbourhood. Satrajit countered these arguments forcefully and received vociferous support from the public galleries. Such was the din that it was difficult to hear Satrajit's words.

'I want Krishna Vaasudeva to tell the Sabha which king from Aryavarta came to our help when Magadha Samrat Jarasandha mounted repeated attacks on Mathura,' Satrajit said and added, 'Things came to such a pass that we, the Yadavas, had to flee from our homeland and relocate to this far-flung Saurashtra coast. Which king came to help us then? We should leave the kings in the north to settle their mutual affairs.

'Instead of needlessly worrying about what is happening in other janapadas, each Yadava must strive for personal betterment, gain more assets and become respected persons in their land. I will go one step further and say that bickerings in Aryavarta will benefit Dwaraka. Those kingdoms will expend their resources in fighting wars, lose men and material. In contrast, Yadavas of Dwaraka, with their focus on improving their lives would become stronger,' he said, looking around with satisfaction at the applause from many in the Sabha.

Krishna's proposal was struck down when a majority of people raised their hands supporting Satrajit's stand against intervention in Pushkar. Krishna bowed his head in acceptance of the Sabha's considered decision.

'Krishna Vaasudeva, is there anything else that you want to place before the Sabha for consideration?' Raja Ugrasena asked.

'Yes, Maharaja! Drupada Maharaja of Panchala has called a swayamvara for his daughter Draupadi. I propose that the Sabha grant permission to Yadava youth desirous of participating in the swayamvara at Kampilya,' Krishna submitted.

This was a non-controversial proposal which could have easily secured the Sabha's nod of approval. However, Satrajit was determined to demonstrate his clout among the Mukhyas. He had come prepared with enough men to object to whatever Krishna said. They all rose to shout Krishna down. Such was the clamour of dissenting voices that the Maharaja rejected the proposal outright, without even putting it to vote. Krishna stood his ground and argued that there was no harm if someone from Dwaraka won the princess's hand at the swayamvara.

The King agreed that there was merit in Krishna's argument. He amended his decision and said Yadavas, if they so desired, could go to Kampilya to attend the swayamvara, but they should not participate in the event.

Krishna once again stood humbled. He bent his head reverentially, accepting the Sabha's decision. Krishna, Satyaki and their supporters left the Sabha with heads bent.

Satrajit was very happy. His clout in the Yadava Mukhyas' Sabha had increased significantly. He derived great satisfaction that this had been proved in the Sabha. He had shown that he could hold against this upstart youth, Krishna. Satrajit's will, regarding what Dwaraka would or would not do, had prevailed.

Satrajit was also surprised. He did not expect his victory to be so easy and smooth. Krishna had accepted the decisions without a fight! It was so unlike Krishna! He had accepted too easily, without any protest! That was uncharacteristic!

Yes, there was something that was not right. The wily cow-grazer had something up his sleeve, Satrajit was convinced. He must continue with his close watch on Krishna and his friends. After all, as a Mukhya of the Sabha, it was his responsibility to ensure that its decisions are complied with. Yes, he must keep tabs on Krishna and his small band of supporters, he decided as he headed homeward.

Meanwhile, he must celebrate his grand victory over Krishna, Satrajit decided as he looked around at the sizeable number of people following him. Food and drinks! Yes, that is the way to enhance one's support base! Yes, he would round off the day with hearty celebrations. There would be more than enough food and drinks for all!

Krishna was disappointed that he was unable to convince his own people in favour of exerting themselves to uphold dharma. More importantly, his plans had received a major setback. Achieving his objectives—setting Pushkar free from foreign occupation and ensuring the successful conduct of the swayamvara at Kampilya— would have been easy enough, if he had Dwaraka's might behind him. That support had been denied to him.

Now he had to work alone to achieve his objectives. He was happy that the Mukhyas' Sabha, while refusing permission for the Yadavas' participation in the swayamvara, had not banned their presence at the event. He would go and assist Draupadi in selecting a suitable groom for herself.

Krishna was particularly disappointed that his own brother did not support him. Yet, he understood why Bhaiya Balarama supported the Pushkar occupation. The eldest of the Kaurava brothers, Duryodhana, had spent some months in Dwaraka, immediately after Yudhishtira was crowned the Yuvaraja of Hastinapura. Duryodhana was a good archer and wanted to hone his skills in fighting with a mace. He chose Balarama as his guru, as he was one of the best in the use of the mace—both for offence and defence. An affectionate bond had developed between the two. Balarama considered his disciple unlucky in being born to a blind father, which denied him his right to become the Yuvaraja.

Satyaki was a pillar of support to Krishna during these trying times. He reached the seafront unfailingly every morning even before Krishna, tried to inspire more young men to join him in fitness training and also to participate in Krishna's mission. Even so, the number of trainees on any given day did not exceed two score.

These rigorous training sessions on the seafront confirmed Satrajit's suspicions that Krishna was up to some mischief. Was Krishna ready to flout the orders of the Mukhyas' Sabha? That would be a crime. As a senior and responsible member of the Sabha, he must ensure proper compliance with the Sabha's decisions by everyone, irrespective of who he is, Satrajit thought and set to work. He mounted a constant vigil on Krishna and ordered his men to keep him informed about every detail of Krishna's activities. Unknown to them, there was another set of men who were also engaged in a similar activity. This band of informers tracked not only Krishna's activities, but also those who kept tabs on Krishna. They reported to someone else.

Krishna and Satyaki decided that they would go ahead with their plan of reaching Kampilya, stopping at Pushkar on the way. According to this plan, Satyaki would lead one part of their delegation early next morning and Krishna would follow exactly a fortnight later. They would meet at Pushkar and travel together to Kampilya.

Late that evening, after their training session wound up for the day, the two friends stayed back to make a final review of the preparations. Krishna felt restless. He needed solitude. He sent Satyaki home telling him to rest before setting out early in the morning, and stayed back by the sea for contemplation.

How lucky he was to have a friend like Satyaki, Krishna thought as he looked at the receding figure of Satyaki. He was a good archer, an able organizer and more than everything else, a staunch friend.

He would have made a good husband to the Panchala princess Draupadi, if only he could participate in the swayamvara.

The thought of Draupadi's swayamvara refreshed memories of his last visit to Panchala. His talk with Drupada was frank and detailed. The king tried to persuade Krishna to wed his daughter. He would give half of his kingdom to Krishna in addition to rebuilding Mathura, the former Yadava homeland destroyed by Jarasandha. He went to the extent of threatening that if Krishna refused his proposal, he would be forced to accept Jarasandha's offer and make his poutra Meghasandhi his son-in-law. On his part, Krishna tried to make the king let go of his enmity towards Drona. When that did not work, Krishna pointed out that the king was being unfair to his daughter by first filling her with hatred and vengeance and now bartering away her life's happiness by making her marry for the wrong reasons.

'You do not know my daughter. Not only is she beautiful, she is a strong-willed person whose commitment to achieving her father's life goal is exemplary,' the king responded, and realizing that Krishna was not convinced, added, 'While it is against royal tradition, I will let you meet my daughter and talk things out with her.'

Draupadi was everything her father said she was. She was open and direct and impressed him with her logic when she spoke about a popularly believed story for the genesis of the Drupada–Drona stand-off. 'It is said that Drona had come seeking a cow so that his only son had enough milk, and a little money for himself. But the Panchala King, not only refused help, but had him chased away. But tell me, will Drupada, whose reputation is that none returns empty handed from him, refuse one cow to his childhood friend? And could his wife Kripi possibly be in such a desperate situation as to have no money even to feed her only son? Kripi, who was brought up by none other than Emperor Shantanu himself? If that is true, then how does it reflect on the Kuru kingdom? This incident left my father completely shaken. Drupada, who had repulsed Jarasandha single-handedly, had lost his confidence. He contemplated suicide. That was when I and my brother, Drishtadyumna, promised to take revenge for his insult. We mean to deliver on our promise. Will you help us or not?'

'Princess, I admire your straightforwardness and courage. But please understand that marriage is not a trade or business. Marriage should be based on mutual respect, love and trust and not for any other consideration; in marriage, everything else, except love and trust, are extraneous. I think you should have the freedom to marry whom you like, independent of your father's need for revenge. Marrying someone with the expectation that he will achieve your objective can spell disaster if, for some reason, that person is unable to measure upto your expectations. Then, you cannot love him, nor can you live in deceit forever.'

Draupadi's assertion that the best archer in Aryavarta was bound to fulfill her objective, gave Krishna an idea. He suggested that Draupadi test her suitors, select the best archer and marry him, irrespective of who he is.' You do this and I promise to stand by you and your father. Please accept me as one of you—your well-wisher,' he said.

With Draupadi agreeing to this proposal, Krishna was able to convince King Drupada to organize a swayamvara for his daughter. 'Organize the swayamvara in its true spirit. Then, Draupadi will have a husband of her choice, who is the best archer in Aryavarta and your prestige will increase. Moreover, since the process of selection is open and transparent, you would not make any enemies,' he said. He assured the help of his guru, Acharya Sandipani, in devising the test for prospective suitors. And, cautioning Drupada to keep the details of the test under wraps till the day of the swayamvara, Krishna took his leave to attend to certain other issues he considered important to resolve this long-standing enmity between Drona and Drupada.

Krishna's satisfaction at the outcome of his Kampilya visit came on top of an entire gamut of emotions he went through at Hastina earlier. When he was setting out, his idea was to guide Yudhishtira in finding his feet as crown prince. Even before he started, news came that the Pandavas were exiled. He set out amidst questions regarding his rationale for the visit to Hastina when Yudhishtira was no longer the Yuvaraja. And then, even as he was still enroute, Bhratvaja Uddhava brought devastating news—all the Pandavas, with their mother Kunti, had perished in a fire accident, their bodies charred beyond recognition. Uddhava was so rattled with this development that he suggested returning to Dwaraka. But Krishna had persisted; he felt he would be able to find clues about the accident at Varanavata. How did such a large fire accident happen! Also, his visit could not be construed as being out of place, for it was the established courtesy for members of a woman's parental home to condole her death with members of her marital home. In this case, Kunti was Vasudeva's sister and Krishna, Vasudeva's son.

It was his first visit to this great kingdom of the Kuru dynasty. He had struck an instant bond of friendship with Bhima and Arjuna, the second and third of the Pandava brothers, when he met them for the first time soon after he joined his biological parents in Mathura. He had an instinctive respect for Yudhishtira, whose commitment to the path of dharma he found highly inspiring. That was a major reason that prompted his decision to be in Hastina as the eldest Pandava brother had learned to navigate his new role as Yuvaraja.

He also developed high regard for Bhishma Pitamaha, whose resolve not to marry on account of a promise he made to his stepmother Satyavati's father, remained unshaken even when Satyavati herself urged him to enter *grihastashram*. He respected the legendary wisdom of Vidura, a son born into the family through a maid and accepted as a younger brother by Bhishma.

During his visit, Krishna had a chance to interact with both Bhishma Pitamaha and Pujyamata Satyavati, in addition to Dhritarashtra, Duryodhana and Shakuni, among others.

Pitamaha's explanation was: 'Rivalries between the sons of Pandu and Dhritarashtra were peaking, and I feared for the safety of the Pandavas. Shakuni was plotting a palace coup to dethrone Yudhishtira. I have toiled all my life to keep the Kuru family united, and was waiting for an opportune time to carve out a small portion of the kingdom for Pandu's sons when this accident happened.'

'Are you convinced that it was an accident?'

The old man shrugged his drooping shoulders. 'They recovered bodies from that house—five male and one female. Duryodhana performed the last rites for the Pandava brothers and Kunti.'

Krishna's expectation of a routine courtesy call on the Pujyamata dissolved into nothingness from the very moment he entered her presence. She lived in a separate palace in the same complex as the rest of the royal family, but spent most of her time in prayer. Krishna was struck by her extraordinarily beautiful looks even at this advanced age, and felt that she took an active interest in the goings on in the family and in the kingdom. His guess proved right when she questioned him closely on his concept of dharma and his priorities in public life. She surprised him a while later, when she disclosed that she, through her trusted aides, had engineered the safe escape of Kunti and her sons from their allotted palace in Varanavata. She had a tunnel dug, which took them to the banks of Ganga, and had them transported to the other bank of the river. 'They must be somewhere in the jungles of Nagakoota. But I dare not send anyone to find them for fear of exposing them to Duryodhana's men,' she said and added, 'Nagakoota is your

Maatamahi's (maternal grandmother Marisha) land. Please find the Pandavas and take them to Dwaraka.'

Krishna lay on the sands, staring into the sky. He wondered if Uddhava, whom he had deputed to Nagakoota, had found anything. Thoughts of what it would be like when the 'dead' Pandavas were found to be alive were taking shape in his mind when sleep claimed his senses.

10

'*Vahni! Jeshtha Bhrata!*'

Rukmini kept calling as she pounded on the front door of Balarama and Revati's living quarters, her voice betraying extreme agitation. She was in total disarray—her untied hair flying in all directions; her veil trailing behind her; her cheeks a burning pink and eyes distraught; face liberally smeared with kohl and tears flowing down her cheeks. Revati, who had never seen Rukmini in such a state, pulled her in and closed the door to avoid gossip, should anyone see Krishna's wife raving and ranting so early in the morning.

'I am ruined! My life is over! I am ruined…ruined…ruined…' Rukmini's high-pitched raving of a while ago had given way to muttering. She had collapsed on the floor and kept shaking her head.

'Calm down, Rukmini, calm down!' Revati ran a reassuring hand over Rukmini's back. 'What happened? Why are you upset?'

Rukmini looked at Revati and her eyes welled afresh. 'I am ruined, Vahni. My life is over. I have nothing to live for. My Prananath has gone away. Left me…left us all and gone away,' she sobbed uncontrollably.

It made no sense to Revati. 'Where has he gone so early in the morning? And why?'

'Revati, what is all that noise? Stop it. Can I not sleep peacefully in my own house?' Balarama shouted from his bedroom, his angry voice heavy with sleep and slurring on account of the heavy dose of wine he had consumed the night before.

The sound jolted Rukmini into action. She rose and rushed into her brother-in-law's bedroom, closely followed by Revati.

'You don't want your sleep disturbed. Sleep; sleep as much as you want; no one will disturb you; your brother Krishna will not disturb you. He will not come to wake you and make you do anything,' Rukmini spluttered.

Balarama realized that something was not right. He sat up, rubbed his eyes and shook his head. 'You...you are Rukmini... Why are you here... Where is Krishna?'

'He has gone...gone away from me...gone away from you... From all of us...gone away from Dwaraka...gone away...gone away...'

'Gone away! Where? Why? Why are you crying?' Balarama strained to understand.

'He has gone away; he will never come back. He left us because we let him down...deceived him. He will not ever come back.' There was anger and despair in Rukmini's voice.

Balarama's patience was wearing thin. He turned to his wife. 'What is this nonsense? Who deceived whom and why go away?'

Revati looked helplessly from one to the other. 'Please Rukmini, collect yourself and tell us exactly what happened!'

Rukmini took a deep breath, wiped her face with the edge of her pallu and looking straight into Balarama's eyes, spoke slowly and clearly, 'This is his message to you. "Bhaiya! I promised Raja Chekitana that I will restore Pushkar to him; I promised Raja Drupada that his daughter's swayamvara will be conducted successfully; I promised Draupadi that I will help her select a brave warrior as husband..."'

Balarama interrupted her, 'Has he nothing better to do than to go about making useless promises? And send his wife over to bother me early in the morning?'

Anger flared in Rukmini again. 'Let me finish reading his message to you. Then you can say and do what you think is right. He said: "I made these promises because I was confident of support from the Yadavas of Dwaraka. But Dwaraka has changed; the Yadavas have changed. So, I will try to fulfill my promises on my own."'

A look of disbelief came into Balarama's eyes. 'And now he has gone to deliver on these impossible, mindless promises?'

'Yes, you refused to help him. All the Yadavas refused to help. So, he had no option but to try and keep his promises solely through his own efforts.'

Balarama clapped his hands in mock appreciation. 'That is great! The great Krishna has taken off to sacrifice himself. Krishna, the hero!'

Rukmini ignored the sarcasm and continued, 'Yes, he will not come back till he fulfils on his promises. And Jeshtha Bhrata, there is one secret message he wanted conveyed only to you: "Bhaiya, I have promised the Pujyamata of Hastina that I will bring out the Pandavas alive at Draupadi's swayamvara in Kampilya."'

Balarama jumped up, lost balance and fell back on his bed. Words failed him. He looked around wildly, then picked up a pitcher of water on his bedside table and poured cold water over his head. 'Revati, I am not sure I heard Rukmini right. Please repeat it for me—slowly and clearly, please!'

Revati spoke like one in a daze, '"I have promised the Pujyamata of Hastina that I will bring out the Pandavas alive at Draupadi's swayamvara in Kampilya."'

Balarama sat down, shaking his head and trying to think cogently. When he spoke, he addressed none in particular and looked at none. He muttered to himself. 'Bring out the Pandavas alive…Pandavas alive… Are they alive? Is it possible?

'But then, Krishna will not make empty promises. If he says he will bring the Pandava brothers alive, there is something to it…something very important! Oh, what have I done! I have let my brother down! I held his hand when he learned to walk, but let him go alone when he wanted to achieve the impossible. He was right; too much wealth is bad, it only leads to indulgence and laziness. If Krishna can really bring the 'dead' brothers to life, and install them on the Hastina throne…what cannot happen! I must help him. Help Krishna with whatever he has planned. I have to change; the Yadavas must change; give up this life of indulgence and return to a disciplined life; only then will they be enabled to think straight and make the correct decisions.'

He had risen and was pacing up and down as he pondered over the situation. He came to a halt in front of Rukmini, who had been helped into an upright posture by Revati. 'I still cannot understand why Krishna left today. As per his plans, Satyaki was to leave this morning with a group of men. Krishna was to follow sometime later. What happened to Satyaki? Has he left Krishna? Has Satyaki run away?'

'Yes, that was the original plan. But no, Satyaki did not run away. He has disappeared. He was probably kidnapped.'

'Rukmini is right. Satyaki is not one to run away. His faith in Krishna is unshakable and he will happily lay down his life for Krishna. So, if he has disappeared, it is only because someone played a dirty trick. He may have been killed,' Revati said.

Balarama flared up in anger. 'Who can stoop to such lowly acts…killing someone because you do not agree with someone else's policies? It can only be that Satrajit. I will get to the bottom of this. I will not let him get away with murder.

'There will be no drinking…no one will touch wine till we punish those responsible for Satyaki's disappearance. We must all help Krishna achieve his objectives,' he declared and stepped out to implement his decisions.

Knowing it was futile, Satyaki made yet another attempt at getting his bearings. There had been no breach in the darkness of the place since he had been dumped there several hours ago. His eyes were quite adjusted to the darkness to perceive even the slightest difference of contour around him. But no, there was no relief. This room—if it was a room—was completely barren. He guessed that he was in an underground dungeon—his conclusion based on the downward movement he felt as he was being carried there by his abductors.

Satyaki made a mental tour of Dwaraka, trying to remember if there was any house with underground cellars. He could recall none, and he knew the city quite well. He then tried to guess who had engineered his kidnapping. It had to be someone who opposed Krishna and his current expedition to Aryavarta.

The identity of the plotter was of little consequence right now, even though he could think of at least five or six persons. Satrajit was not in this list. He was, after all, a Mukhya and generally not given to underhand dealings.

He needed to get out and commence the journey he was to start at daybreak that day. Satyaki knew that the scheduled moment of his departure was long past. He was about six hours from that time when he left Krishna on the sea shore and headed home. He estimated that he had been here for well over twelve hours.

What would have happened to the small contingent that he was to have led? Would they have left under some other leader? More importantly, what would Krishna have thought about his absence? Oh! I have let Krishna down! Let him down when he needed support more than ever before! He was facing a lot of opposition from various quarters. Wealth and prosperity had made the Yadavas lazy, indolent and selfish. They had forgotten that it was Krishna's efforts and initiatives that had enabled the Yadavas to be what they were today. And he, the son of Satyaka Mukhya, who knew it all and was ready to give his all to help Krishna, had been taken out of action by his opponents.

Satyaki became alert as he picked up the muted sounds of approaching footsteps. With his hands tied behind his back, he knew he could only use his full body weight to throw his captors off balance. 'If only he knew where to pounce,' he thought. A small square patch opened in the roof and a stepladder was lowered. The light was hardly any better.

'Climb.'

The simple order stunned Satyaki. Whatever he had been expecting, it was definitely not a feminine voice. Had he been kidnapped by a woman? No! He had been ambushed by more than one person and handled by more than one person. They were all men; he was sure!

'Quick,' the second and equally terse order commanded immediate action and Satyaki obeyed. He had no option.

He emerged into a low-ceilinged tunnel, where he could hardly stand straight. He followed the woman whose head was covered. It was a short walk and the tunnel opened into a room where he could stand straight and there was better light.

The woman who led him now turned. Satyaki recognized her. She was the daughter of Satrajit. Anger flared when he noticed a happy grin on the girl's face.

'I knew that Satrajit is a mean, selfish man who will stoop to any level to discredit Krishna. But I could never imagine that his daughter would also be bad. You are a blot on the fair name of women. What harm has Krishna done to you that you should participate in this nefarious design to foil Krishna's noble mission?' Satyaki could not use harsh words against women, but neither could he remain silent in the face of such a provocative act.

'I am glad that you have recognized me, but that is hardly the proper way to thank me for saving your life.' The girl continued to smile happily.

'You! You saved my life! Do you think I am a fool to believe you? Your father hates Krishna. He always did. And you, his daughter, cannot be different. You support your father and his ambition, and so you prevented me from going on my expedition this morning,' Satyaki had difficulty controlling his temper.

'Stop! That is enough! I will not stand here listening to you say nasty things about my father. And believe me when I tell you that there was a plan to get you killed, but my father had nothing to do with it. I intervened and saved you.'

'If that is so, perhaps you will also tell me why you saved me. What is your interest in me?'

She laughed, 'You flatter yourself, Yuyudhana, by thinking I have any interest in you. My interest is not in you, but in Krishna. I know that he is planning an extraordinary feat. He needs you; you can help him achieve his objective. Also, I do not want him to face such danger alone. So I went to great trouble to plan this operation to save you.'

Satyaki was confused. 'But your father is against Krishna. I know that Satrajit is jealous of Krishna—jealous that he is loved and respected, that his views count in the Sabha of Mukhyas. That is why he opposes everything proposed by Krishna, tries to put spokes in every mission Krishna undertakes.'

'I agree. But I will also say that my father is a good human being, and insist that wanting power commensurate with his standing and ability is no crime.'

'Ha! What ability are you talking about? Tell me one single occasion when he was able to foil Krishna's plans!'

'I pity you, Yuyudhana! The reason for my father's failure is not his lack of capability, but because I have worked overtime to ensure Krishna's success. I sabotage my father's plans to ensure Krishna's success. I have also made it my business to maintain a generous supply of horses, chariots and gold for Krishna's missions. All these belong to my father. I steal them for Krishna.' There was a hint of pride in her voice.

Satyaki felt overwhelmed. Satyabhama's disclosures were hard for an already tired and tense mind. Lack of sleep and food complicated the situation further, and he felt weak. He leaned against a nearby pillar for support. His head was spinning, he could hardly think cogently. Something was still not right!

'If what you say is true, why did you keep me locked up the whole day?' he asked and continued without waiting for her reply. 'Anyway, that is immaterial. I have lost enough time already. I must go. I have to be on my way.'

'Do not be a fool. There is a good reason why I could not free you earlier. I will tell you the details while you get some food in you,' Satyabhama brought out a plate full of fruits. 'Eat!' she commanded as she untied his hands.

'I have readied a chariot with four well-trained horses and an able charioteer. You should cross the outskirts of Dwaraka in the darkness of night so that you are not discovered. Then, you will be able to catch up with Krishna when they stop for the night tomorrow.'

'What! Where has Krishna gone?'

'Oh! I forgot that you did not know what happened this morning! Oh! There was chaos when you went missing! There were people all over. There was so much talk, so much gossip,' Satyabhama's voice thrilled with excitement.

She continued, 'Krishna took your place and led the march. My messengers informed me that Krishna said that you were in some trouble and had not deserted as alleged by some. He changed the original plan and said that the other group, which was to leave with him in a fortnight, should leave in three days and catch up with him. Then, he went home, picked up his bow, *chakra* and conch, and left.

'I went out then to assess the situation so that I could set you on your way as soon as possible. I saw Rukmini running towards Balarama's quarters. Oh, she was a sight to see! I followed her and was hiding behind a bush when she screamed at Balarama.

'Balarama came on to his terrace after a while. He was drenched, water dripping from his head. He blew his conch and announced that he will lead the second group on the appointed day. He ordered people to give up wine and train hard so that they could help Krishna.

'The city burst into activity almost immediately—some rushed to King Ugrasena to have a Mukhyas' Sabha convened, some went about trying to find out what happened to you, and some went to bring young men to the seafront to start training exercises.

'I could not risk your being seen by anyone. So I waited till dusk to get you out. You still have some time before starting. Eat well and shore up your energies.'

Satyaki was filled with gratitude for Satyabhama, whom he always considered an adversary along with her father. 'I do not know how I can repay your kindness, Satya. I still cannot believe that Krishna has such an ardent follower in Satrajit's family.'

'You and I have a lot of similarities, Yuyudhana. I hope you don't mind my calling you by the name given to you rather than "Satyaki" after your father. Initially, you chose to stand against Krishna because you considered him a rival in the race to the top. That was why you made common cause with my father. But you demonstrated the courage to correct your misconceptions and become the right-hand man of the same Krishna. And I grew up hearing a lot of negative things about Krishna. I started to observe Krishna, understand his point of view and compare it with how he was being portrayed by my father. I liked him so much that I wanted to be his wife. I confess to being heartbroken when Krishna married Rukmini. A princess is not the right wife for Krishna, because the royalty has strict notions about conduct. They are stiff and cold. Krishna is fun-loving. I will be a better wife to him. He will be mine. People will forget all the songs about the love of all the gopikas of Vrindavan for Krishna.

'You spoke about repaying my kindness, Yuyudhana. Be my friend and, at the right time, help me achieve my objective. I will ensure that Krishna becomes "Satya-Pati",' she said with a proud toss of her head.

❧

Krishna looked around, his eyes showing a hint of anxiety. The huge pandal, specially erected on the palace grounds for Draupadi's swayamvara, was already buzzing with activity. The arrangements were elaborate and impeccable. There was a high podium from where the King of Panchala, Drupada, would preside over the proceedings. There was an elaborate *yagnakund* one step lower and Brahmin priests were chanting *mantras* and feeding the fire in the yagnakund. A sitting enclosure for the bride-to-be and her *sakhis*, or companions, was located near the yagnakund.

At a level further lower was the arena where the invitees would be tested as per the rules of the swayamvara. It was Draupadi's desire to wed an expert archer. A bejewelled but unstrung bow was placed on a pedestal. Next to the bow were five flower-tipped arrows. The target, a fish, had been fitted into a circular frame that was mounted on a long staff. The staff itself was fitted in the middle of a small pond. The circular frame with the target rotated at varying speeds. Suitors were required to pierce it with an arrow by looking at its reflection in the pond. Draupadi would marry the winner of this test.

Acharya Sandipani, who devised the test and his assistant Swetaketu, who supervised its setting up, were also the designated judges for the swayamvara and had their seats close to the pond.

Invitee galleries were arranged in a semicircle around the three-tier structure. Here too, there were separate enclosures for each of the invited guests and their delegations. Coupled with the mounting buzz of anticipation and exchange of greetings among the guests, was a general air of surprise and nervousness. Invitees were informed of the test only on the eve of the swayamvara, and several guests knew that they had no chance of victory in this complicated test.

Krishna looked around the galleries yet again and seemed disappointed. The enclosures for Brahmins and Kshatriyas were the target of his scrutiny.

All eyes turned to the main entrance as Draupadi, escorted by her brother Drishtadyumna, entered the hall. She walked slowly, with eyes demurely lowered and with a green coconut in her hands. She first went to her father to seek his blessings. She then walked down to where Acharya Sandipani was seated and walked round the pond thrice before touching the Acharya's feet reverentially. She then walked up to the middle level, handed over the coconut to the chief priest and occupied the seat meant for her. Her sakhis formed a protective ring around her, some seated on stools and the others standing. A large ornate tray with a flower garland was placed on a nearby table.

Krishna looked at the radiantly beautiful Draupadi, dressed in royal finery and adorned with jewellery and flowers. She seemed happy. 'I hope she finds her ideal companion through this swayamvara and lead a happy life', Krishna thought, even as his eyes scanned several enclosures once again. His eyes lit up as he found what he was seeking. He tapped on Balarama's shoulder, and with his eyes, pointed to the object of his satisfaction.

Balarama looked, and his eyes dancing with joy, put a loving arm around his younger brother. 'How did you manage this miracle, Kanha? After all, it is not easy to bring back the dead.'

'No, Bhaiya, there is no miracle. They had all escaped.'

'How? How can that be? Duryodhana is said to have performed the last rites for the deceased brothers and their mother. Their charred bodies were there; they were found! How can you explain that?' Balarama asked.

Krishna smiled and glanced at the Pandavas, dressed as Brahmin youths. He then began to satiate his brother's curiosity, even as he kept an eye on the proceedings in the swayamvara arena, 'Bhaiya, there was enough to suspect foul play when the Pandavas were directed to this palace in Varanavata, constructed specially for their exile. These suspicions strengthened when Duryodhana appointed an officer to look after them and the palace was found to have been painted with inflammable substances like shellac.'

'Then why did they stay there? They could have easily gone away to a safer place,' Balarama interjected.

'True. But then, what is the guarantee that Duryodhana will not devise another, more dangerous plot to get them killed? So, Vidura advised them to continue there, remaining alert at all times. Vidura deployed his own men to keep tabs on Duryodhana's officer and dig a secret tunnel to a designated place in the jungles along the banks of Ganga. Vidura and Pujyamata Satyavati worked together to ensure the safety of the Pandavas. They even arranged for duplicate bodies to be placed in the palace, when needed. A boat was ready to transport them to the other bank in the dark of night.

'These jungles abut Nagakoota. The Nagas of these jungles are cannibals and eat humans who stray into their territory. The Pandavas had to deal with this danger on their own, and that was a reason of worry for Pujyamata. Also, there was no way to contact them or send messages to them on account of the elaborate spy networks established by Duryodhana and Shakuni.

'Pujyamata asked me to find the Pandavas and take them to Dwaraka for their safety. I sent Uddhava to scout for them, but did not like the idea of relocating them in Dwaraka, because then, they would have to live their lives incognito and fall prey to Duryodhana's plots sooner or later.

'The Pandavas are great warriors and committed to treading the path of dharma. They must be in a position from where they can shape the destiny of mankind. So, I told Uddhava to bring them here today and have them disclose themselves in the swayamvara arena in front of this large assemblage of kings. Then, none can deny their being alive and Duryodhana cannot get away with murder.'

Balarama looked with admiration at his brother, holding him close with one arm. Both brothers shifted their attention to the proceedings in the swayamvara arena.

The competition had begun and several suitors were unable to even string the bow. Krishna stole a glance at Duryodhana and noted that he was following the proceedings with keen interest, possibly assessing the toughness of the task and devising his own strategy. Krishna knew that the eldest Kuru prince wished to win the hand of the Panchala princess, and with help of Panchala, challenge the Magadha emperor Jarasandha. Duryodhana was a capable archer, even though his prowess could not compare with that of Arjuna or Karna. Karna, who was in the same enclosure, was equally keen to win Draupadi's hand; as that would scale up his social status.

Krishna stole a look at his brother's profile and knew that he was torn between two competing emotions. Balarama had particular affection for Duryodhana, who had tutored under him in mace-combat. It was natural, therefore, for Balarama to wish for Duryodhana's success. However, for the larger good of the entire region, he knew that Arjuna needed to participate in the swayamvara and win Draupadi's hand.

Even as Balarama struggled with these competing wishes, Duryodhana entered the arena, and inexplicably, failed to even string the bow. He tripped and fell back, dislodging his crown in the process. That was a humiliation for the Hastina Yuvaraja, who was helped back to his seat by an aide. Karna faced a similar humiliation when he was declared ineligible to contest on account of his lower social status by birth.

A wave of murmuring arose in the hall as the swayamvara's collapse seemed imminent. In that case, the princess could, if she so chose, select her mate from among the invitees, bypassing the contest.

A sudden hush fell over the gathering as a Brahmin youth approached Drupada for permission to compete. Even before the confusion over this unexpected entrant stilled, the youth had not only stringed the bow, but pierced the fish rotating high above.

The four brothers of the winner jumped into the arena and disclosed their identity. News that the Pandavas were alive created a pandemonium. Almost everybody in every enclosure was standing up, trying to take a good look at the man who won the seemingly impossible test. Speculation regarding the identity of the winner dominated the chatter. Could it really be Pandava Madhyama Arjuna? Were the Pandavas not dead? But of course they were dead! Their last rites were duly performed by Duryodhana. Some disciples of Acharya Sandipani and Acharya Swetaketu, sitting far away from the podium, worried that a Brahmin youth could be declared ineligible to wed a Kshatriya princess.

Duryodhana alone sat still in his seat. He did not need to look at the winner or need help to know the winner's identity. He could only be the Pandava Madhyama Arjuna. In fact, he had suspected their presence even as he was attempting a hit at the *matsya-yantra*. He had heard derisive laughter, which he dismissed at that time as a figment of his imagination. Even then he had known that it was Bhima's laughter. How had they escaped the shellac palace in Varanavata? If they had got away, how did he find six bodies in the burnt down palace?

His lips twisted in a wry smile when he noticed, even without really looking, that Krishna and Balarama had rushed into the middle of the hall to embrace the Pandavas disguised as Brahmin youths. Of course it had to be the doing of that wily Yadava. He was blatantly partisan and promoted the Pandava cause at his expense. Bad luck never left him; it always came in the way of him getting his due.

Acharya Sandipani, assisted by his numerous disciples, managed to restore a semblance of order and announced the result of the matsya-yantra test, 'The winner is from the Kuru Vamsa, poutra of Santanu Chakravarti of Hastinapura, and putra of Maharaja Pandu, Arjuna.'

The assembly once again erupted into a buzz of voices marvelling at the re-emergence of the Pandavas, who were believed to have been killed in a fire accident more than a year ago. People pointed fingers at the towering personality of Bhima and said he could not be mistaken; he could be none other than Bhima. And the others too were recognizable as the other Pandava brothers. How did they escape death? Was the accident engineered by the Kauravas? There was enough evidence to believe that. Was not Hastinapura full of rumours of differences between the cousins?

Acharya Sandipani's disciples walked around the various enclosures urging them to be seated and let the proceedings of the day's contest reach their logical conclusion. Acharya Sandipani escorted the winner to the Panchala King for proper introductions. Acharya Swetaketu escorted the princess up the podium, her sakhis following them with the *jayamala* on a tray. Draupadi knelt at her father's feet for his blessings and allowed him to help her up and place the garland around Arjuna's neck.

❧

D waraka was in turmoil.

Krishna was dead.

Public verdict was unanimous—Satrajit was guilty; he was squarely to be blamed for it.

Everyone knew why and how it happened. It all happened because of the Syamantaka *mani,* or gem.

The Syamantaka had magical powers and it belonged to Satrajit.

He came to possess this wondrous gem by accident. He chanced upon it while on a business trip across the high seas, and he purchased it on impulse. As much by chance, while still on the trip, he learnt that the gem had miraculous powers. It could produce huge quantities of gold every day.

Satrajit was very happy. It was sheer luck that brought this gem to him. He spent the gold lavishly to enlarge his clout. He targeted the youth and managed to gain their trust and support. Greater influence among the people translated into more power in the Sabha of Yadava Mukhyas. In effect, he used the mani and the gold it produced to build a strong anti-Krishna base under his leadership.

It was therefore not surprising that Satrajit perceived an ulterior purpose in Krishna's proposal that he hand over the Syamantaka to King Ugrasena. Krishna had argued that the Syamantaka had powers other than producing gold. It had medicinal and occult powers, which could become available to the entire population only if it was in the king's custody. Placing the gem in the king's authority would also prevent its misuse.

Satrajit vehemently opposed the proposal. He had procured the gem through his personal efforts and thus had full rights over it. The king could only lay claim to a small part of any benefits that accrue to the people through governmental efforts, but could not confiscate the personal assets of any citizen. When more people advocated the gem's transfer to the kingdom's treasury, Satrajit threatened armed resistance.

Krishna's Pitruvya, Akrura, found Satrajit's threat of armed resistance unacceptable and dangerous. And he joined Krishna on his visits to Satrajit. His position as a co-Mukhya in the Sabha, his stature as an elder statesman and comparable age made for better chances of success. Akrura initially tried to reason with Satrajit and pointed out that individual wealth and skills all belonged to the kingdom and could be requisitioned by the king at any time. In any janapada, there would be several people with different and specialized skills. These skills were to be used for the kingdom's improvement and remain at its command at all times.

In fact, Dwaraka, the Yadava homeland, actually belonged to Balarama. The city, known earlier as 'Kushasthali', was a gift to the elder son of Vasudeva from his Swasura Raivata. 'You may also recall that Balarama had won it for Raja Raivata, and he, in gratitude, had given his daughter Revati to Balarama in marriage. Krishna and Balarama had toiled to develop it and then handed it over to Raja Ugrasena, respecting the decision of the Mukhyas,' he said.

Satrajit remained adamant. 'It is my personal property and I will do whatever is necessary to protect my assets. I have more horses, elephants and heads of cattle than all of you put together. I can protect myself even if the King's army attacks me,' he said.

'A threat of armed struggle against the king is a punishable offence. It will be dealt with,' Krishna warned, and said he knew how to make Satrajit part with the gem.

Several other Mukhyas who tried to reason with Satrajit, also failed. These attempts, however, convinced Satrajit that the Syamantaka was in danger of either being stolen or taken forcibly from him. He discussed the issue with his younger brother Prasena, and decided that it should never be left unguarded. They had it embedded in a frame attached to a gold chain, and either brother would wear it at all times.

One day, Prasena decided to go hunting. Given the Syamantaka's great powers, he wanted to wear it on his hunting trip. 'It will bring me luck. I will return with a great game,' he pleaded with his brother. He did not return. Satrajit sent a search party for Prasena and the Syamantaka. The search failed. Neither was found. Satrajit recalled Krishna's words that he knew how to take the gem from him if he did not give it willingly, and said that Krishna had killed Prasena to steal the Syamantaka.

Krishna and Balarama met Satrajit to tell him that they had nothing to do with Prasena's disappearance. 'We were very much in Dwaraka that entire day,' they explained, but failed to convince the suspicious Satrajit. The two sons of Vasudeva could not take this allegation on their fair name and decided to search the forest for Prasena. 'I will not set foot in Dwaraka without information about Prasena and the Syamantaka,' Krishna vowed.

Balarama and Krishna set out on the mission, and discovered a decomposed and mutilated body. The man had obviously been killed by a wild animal. There was a trail of blood from this body and the trail led to another dead body. This was a lion, which indicated that the lion itself had been killed by another wild beast. There was a further trail of blood from the dead lion, and this trail disappeared into a cave.

It was very dark inside the cave. Krishna tried many tricks to make any animal that might be inside to come out. Nothing worked. 'I swore that I will not enter Dwaraka without the Syamantaka. There is a trail suggesting that the mani could have been taken into this cave by whichever beast that killed the lion. I will go inside and check,' Krishna said.

He told Balarama that he should wait for him for two weeks, and return home if he failed to come out. On the third day after Krishna entered the cave, Balarama heard grunting sounds indicative of an ongoing fight. He concluded that Krishna had come across some beast and was fighting it. It was only a matter of time that Krishna would emerge, possibly with the Syamantaka in his hand.

This, however, did not happen. There was no sign of Krishna and in due course, sounds of combat ceased. Balarama's worst fears had come true. Krishna had been killed inside this cave. Yet, he waited till the end of the fortnight set by Krishna before turning homeward with a heavy heart.

Another fortnight passed, without any trace of Krishna. Public opinion in Dwaraka, which initially gave credence to Satrajit's claims of Krishna's guilt in his brother's murder and theft of the Syamantaka, quickly turned against him. Satrajit was now seen as the villain who pushed an innocent Krishna into the jaws of death by making baseless allegations.

So much so that Satrajit could not step out of the safety of his home. He was scared that, should he be seen on the streets of Dwaraka, he would be lynched by angry mobs. His palatial house, which used to be a teeming hub of activity, was now deserted. Hardly anyone visited the Yadava Mukhya.

While his image in Dwaraka swung from a villain to victim, Krishna was fighting for his life inside the cave. It was pitch dark inside and Krishna took each step carefully, keeping one hand on the wall of the cave for guidance. As he moved deeper and deeper into the cave, Krishna perceived a ray of bright red light from afar. He moved in the direction of the light and in due course, reached its source. Krishna recognized it as the Syamantaka, as its brightness was not on account of reflected light but due to light generated internally. He reached out to take it, when suddenly someone pounced on him from behind and tried to strangle him.

Krishna managed to turn in time to engage the attacker. The two fought, each trying to pin the other down. Neither showed signs of fatigue and they wrestled on for days and weeks. Krishna realized that he was fighting a bear, which had killed the lion and taken the Syamantaka.

He was determined to fight the bear to the finish and take back the gem. He had to return it to Satrajit and clear his name of baseless allegations. Initially, the strength and stamina of his opponent surprised Krishna. The bear seemed to be much larger than an average one. Then, in a flash, he recognized him.

This was Jambavanta, the King of bears. He was a blessed soul and had the strength of a million lions. Brahma had also decreed that Jambavanta would meet his end only at the hands of Vishnu. Jambavanta was a master strategist and was on hand in the Treta Yuga to help Rama in his battle against Ravana. But for the boon that he could be killed only by a *nara* or *vanara*, Ravana would have surely met his end in Jambavanta's hands.

After the battle, Shree Rama thanked Jambavanta for his help and offered him a boon. Jambavanta said that he had never come across a strong opponent to fight against in his entire life and that he would enjoy a good fight with a worthy opponent like Rama. Vishnu avatar Rama had then promised that his desire would be fulfilled in his next incarnation in Dwapara Yuga. 'I will defeat you in the fight and release you from this mortal body.'

With this realization, Krishna continued to give an exhilaratingly tough fight to Jambavanta in the darkness of the cave. They pummelled each other for 28 days without pausing for a break. Both were badly hurt and bled from the numerous wounds they inflicted on each other.

Jambavanta too was surprised at the power of his opponent. When he first pounced on the intruder into his cave, he thought that this average human would fall with just a couple of blows. But when he put up a commendable fight, Jambavanta was filled with admiration. He was really enjoying the combat, the likes of which he had never experienced in his life.

After more than three weeks, Jambavanta's strength gave way. Just as he was giving up, his mind threw up a memory that cleared his doubts about his opponent's identity. Jambavanta had just been flung to the floor and Krishna was about to jump on his chest. Jambavanta rolled over and clutched the Lord's feet. 'Oh, you have come, Shree Rama! I am truly blessed. You have come for me. Rama, I have been waiting for you for so long,' he folded his hands in salutation.

Krishna smiled as he crouched beside the fallen beast. 'Jambavanta, you seem to have lost track of time. I was Rama in Treta Yuga, and now even the next Yuga, Dwapara, is also coming to an end. I am here on earth this time as Krishna.'

'I am honoured, Prabhu! My reunion with you is long overdue. I have grown old and am tired of life. Please tell me what took you so long to bestow your grace on this devotee, and the reason why you came now.'

'Jambavanta, the right time has to come for anything to happen. Also, when in human form, my consciousness surfaces only on occasions when it is necessary. When I entered this cave, I was unaware of the purpose for which I came. I entered this pitch-dark cave looking for this mani that you have hung from the ceiling. It is the Syamantaka mani. I need to return this magical gem to its owner to clear my name of theft and murder.'

'Please take it. Along with this gem, may I present you with another jewel—my daughter. Please accept her. She is standing there in the corner like a frightened doe.'

Krishna looked at the young girl and laughed, 'Jambavanta! You had been a strict brahmachari (celibate) all your life. I am surprised that you let go of this tough *vrata*, or vow, at this late age and entered grihastashram.'

Jambavanta joined the laughter, even though it appeared to increase his bodily pain. 'No, Prabhu, that is not how I got my daughter. She is a gift left in my care by her parents. I went out of my cave on hearing their cries and saw that they were being attacked by a herd of lions. I pushed them away, but the couple was already dead. I brought this baby in and raised her like my own daughter. I have told her that Shree Rama will come to take care of her. I can leave my body if you promise to love and cherish her like I have done. Please Prabhu, promise me; promise that you will not desert her. She is a pious girl, who only knows to love you.'

'I promise, Jambavanta. I will take her with me and marry her in front of my entire family. But tell me, what is her name?'

'She is Jambavanta's daughter. So she is Jambavati,' he said and breathed his last.

❧

14

Satyabhama sat motionless. Neither the chirping of birds, nor the pollen-scented breeze gladdened her overburdened heart. She had lost interest in everything. She had skipped lunch—because she could not bear her father's company; she could not indulge in inane conversations. She had been sitting under a tree in the courtyard; she did not know for how long. She did not care.

Krishna had married again; got himself a second wife. What did he see in her! She is nothing more than an uncouth girl with no knowledge of anything in the world! And what an outlandish name she has—Jambavati! She has no great lineage to boast of. No one even knows who or what her parents were! And brought up by a bear in a dark forest cave! What is her qualification to become Krishna's wife? How did Krishna agree to marrying her?

And Rukmini? Satyabhama could not believe that Rukmini welcomed Jambavati with open arms. In fact, all through the days and weeks when everyone in Dwaraka worried for Krishna, she was calm; as calm as water in a pond. Satyabhama's spy network provided enough evidence that Rukmini was sanguine at all times. She was the one who was consoling Devaki and Vasudeva, Krishna's distraught parents, that there was nothing to worry about. 'Krishna will come to no harm,' she would tell each and everyone who voiced apprehensions for Krishna's safety.

As for the speculations about the success of his mission,

Rukmini would declare, 'He will come back with the gem. In fact, he will return with two gems.'

Satya had scoffed at this prophecy at the time. 'Rukmini is hoping that Krishna will bring a second Syamantaka for her, so that she will also have immense riches,' she had thought. The real meaning of Rukmini's statement—that she referred to Jambavati as the second gem—dawned on her much later.

Satyabhama was jolted out of her reverie when she felt a hand on her shoulder and turned to see her father settling down on the grass beside her. She noticed, for the first time in several weeks, that her father had lost a lot of weight. There were dark circles under his eyes—a sure sign that he was not sleeping well—and he looked old. It was as if he had aged suddenly. The furore over the Syamantaka had left Satrajit friendless. No one visited him; no one consulted him for anything; their home, which used to be full of people visiting them at all times, had fallen silent. And it was an eerie silence, not a peaceful, serene and welcome silence. In fact, on the rare occasions that Satrajit stepped out of his palace, no one greeted him; no one even looked at him; his overtures for interaction only earned him negativity and accusations for having sacrificed Krishna for his selfish ends.

There was no change in the situation even after Krishna returned. None of Satrajit's friends returned to him. Krishna had come and placed the Syamantaka in Satrajit's hand almost immediately after reaching Dwaraka. 'I stand cleared of the stigma of your accusation,' he had said. Krishna did not even stop to be thanked. He just turned on his heel and walked away, even as Satrajit opened his mouth to offer the Syamantaka as a gift to Krishna.

The Syamantaka failed to cheer Satrajit. It was this mani that was at the root of all his present problems. His hope that Krishna would accept the Syamantaka and that it could somehow wipe off the negativity he had earned among the Yadavas had been dashed. Satrajit sorely missed his younger brother Prasena. 'He would have found a way out; he would have helped me take proper decisions,' he thought.

It was an impossible situation. He could not cope with this social boycott. He had to find a way out and regain his place and position in Dwaraka. Satrajit then remembered—Krishna had first suggested that he should handover the Syamantaka to the king. He would do that, he decided, and immediately acted on it. Unfortunately for him, Ugrasena was in no mood to accept the gift. 'I have never sought it and I will not take it now after all that has happened,' he had said.

Satrajit looked at his daughter's profile as she sat staring into the distance. His heart twitched in pain—was this his lovely and vivacious daughter, whose laughter lit up his life? How pale she looked! Her eyes, so full of mischief and zest for life, were now lacklustre! Her thick, long and black hair which touched her knees even when plaited, which Satyabhama herself considered the highlight of her beauty, now lay in an untidy knot at the nape of her neck, completely unadorned and unkempt! What had happened!

'Please tell me what I should do, Satya. I cannot bear to see you unhappy. I offered the Syamantaka to Krishna. He refused it. I offered it to the king. He also did not take it, what can I do?' Satrajit asked, looking closely at his daughter for some reaction. There was none.

Suddenly, an idea struck Satrajit and his face brightened. 'Suppose I offer you along with the Syamantaka to Krishna, perhaps he will agree. Like Jambavanta…Krishna has married Jambavati and taken the gem from Jambavanta.' He looked at his daughter's immobile and expressionless face and hesitatingly asked, 'Will you be agreeable to that, dear?'

Satyabhama turned slowly to face her father. 'The question, Pitashree, is not whether I am agreeable or not, but whether Krishna agrees to it or not.'

Satrajit winced. 'Why will he not agree? Actually, but for this unfortunate incident of the gem, he would not even dare to look at you,' he said.

'Do not underestimate people, Pitashree! You think he is beneath you socially. But think, if he was not great, really great, why did the King of Panchala offer his daughter Draupadi and half his kingdom to Krishna? It was an offer that most kings of Aryavarta would have jumped at. But Krishna refused.

'Let us put our pride aside and take an objective view of our situation. My father is not a king like Rukmini's father. My father is not a consistent and committed devotee like Jambavati's father. And me! I am too proud; I cannot surrender to him like Rukmini. So, do we have the good fortune to even think of Krishna? Think, Pitashree, think.'

Satrajit looked at his daughter in amazement. 'How do you know so much about Krishna? These thoughts have not occurred to me even once. I never knew to look at issues from this perspective,' he said.

'I know, Pitashree! Our perceptions arise from our egos. For some, Krishna is Viswachaitanya—the ultimate beauty and bliss. For others, he is a sworn enemy, an obstacle in progressing on their chosen path.

'What Krishna is to Rukmini, Devaki and Draupadi, he is not for Rukmi, Shishupala or Jarasandha. Only people who can rise above their egos, recognize Krishna as *sarvantaryami*—omnipresent and omniscient. He cannot be lured by beauty or wealth.'

'Why did you not say all this to me earlier? I would have changed my views about him and dealt with issues differently,' Satrajit said, bewildered at the profundity in his daughter's words.

'A fruit separates from the tree only when it is fully ripe. Similarly, human beings see light only when their egos are subdued.

'All of us in our family were hitherto drunk on the power of money. The Syamantaka was everything to us. We invited enmity with all for it. But see what has happened now. Today, the gem's worth is not the same for us. You are ready to give it to Krishna for his friendship. But he does not want it. He went to great lengths, took great trouble to retrieve it. He brought it and returned it to you. So, you see, the gem which can produce huge quantities of gold everyday, did not mean anything to him. It has no takers today. And we, who have it, have no friends. We are ready to exchange it for people's goodwill and friendship. It has lost its worth in our eyes. Now, it is merely a shiny stone! If somebody had said these very words to us some time back, we would have called them names. But today, we know! We know what its worth is!'

Satrajit's jaw dropped. A new realization dawned on him. 'Do you love him, Satya?' he asked.

Satya smiled. It was the smile of wisdom. 'He is Purushottama. He is the dream of every girl. But only a very few lucky ones can get him. You see, Pitashree, Draupadi wanted him. But all the riches of Panchala could not secure him for her. Rukmini loved him enough to let go of all her royal riches. She became his wife.

'You lost the Syamantaka, and accused him of stealing it. As a consequence, Jambavati, without even aspiring for him, became his wife.'

'What about you?'

She looked him straight in the eye. 'I lack maturity. I am also very proud—proud about our wealth, my beauty... No, Pitashree,

I stand no chance. I can never aspire for Krishna's love.'

Satrajit felt her pain. He stood up and pulled Satyabhama to her feet. He steered her indoors, keeping a firm grip on her hand. When he spoke, there was a new determination in his voice. 'My daughter is the best. She deserves the best. She will get the best,' he said.

'Bhama, are you angry with me?' Krishna's voice was a tantalizing mix of love, concern and contriteness.

Satyabhama turned her head and looked at him, her eyes conveying her question. The newly-wed couple was in a palace readied for Krishna's third wife. It was a tastefully decorated palace, thanks mainly to Rukmini's organizing skills. Krishna's *Patta Mahishi* (principal queen) had taken on the responsibility of domestic administration, including the setting up of living quarters for Krishna's other wives. While Jambavati was pleased with the arrangements, Satyabhama was quick to order major alterations in her palace. Gone were all the decorations with any hint of a peacock feather in them—her reason was that she did not want anything to distract her husband's attention; she should be the centre of all his love and attention.

Satyabhama positioned swings strategically all around her palace—in the garden, on the porch, by the pool and so on. Right now, Satyabhama and Krishna were rocking gently on a swing on the porch after dinner, enjoying a cool summer breeze.

Krishna reached out and held her hand in both of his. 'I did not thank you.'

'Thank me! For what?' Satyabhama could not hide her surprise.

'For saving Satyaki. You not only saved his life, but saved my mission,' he said, kissing her hand lightly.

'Then you have to say thanks many more times, you know!' her provocative laughter invited a series of kisses, this time on the palm of her hand, even as he looked questioningly at her.

Satyabhama pulled her hand away. She felt impelled to educate her husband about herself. 'Draupadi's swayamvara is not the only mission of yours that I have saved. In fact, I have contributed to the success of each and every mission of yours.' She responded with tinkling laughter when Krishna raised his brows in surprise and inquiry. 'I used to contribute horses, chariots and gold everytime you set out on any mission.'

'Thank you. I am impressed, intrigued and obliged. May I ask how you managed the donations and from where you got the resources for it,' Krishna asked, quite seriously.

Her reply was equally serious. 'Do not underestimate my organizing capabilities, *Patidev*! I had an elaborate network of informers who would tell me about your plans and movements, and I would make my contributions in small bits through a number of people. As to how I got them, I stole them from my father, thanks to all the gold given by the Syamantaka. I operated in such a manner that my father never got to know.

'I would also have you know, Giridhari, that I can handle horses, manage a chariot, string a bow...' Satyabhama's voice faltered as Krishna moved closer to her on the swing and cupped her face in both his hands. 'Why did you learn them?' he breathed into her ear.

'Because all my help to you till now was indirect. I wanted to be of more direct help to you.' She withdrew from him, putting a cushion between them. 'But tell me, Giridhari, why did you refuse the Syamantaka mani?'

'Because I was interested in this mani,' Krishna said, putting an arm around his wife.

'You already have two manis. So tell me, which mani do you like best?'

Krishna laughed. It was a soft sound, yet carried a shade of seriousness in it. 'You should never make such comparisons. Each jewel is special in its own way, and adorn the same neck.'

'But you must admit that some are brighter than others. So is it not possible that the brightest of all is more important than the others,' Satyabhama persisted, keen to hear something more favourable about herself; something that would emphasize her importance as compared to his other two wives.

'Bhama, it is true that no two manis can be the same. But once they are threaded into one necklace, they all acquire an equal status.'

Satyabhama gave up. She realized that it was not possible to make her husband say what she wanted to hear. She changed the topic. 'There is something that always intrigued me—your refusal to become king. Not once but on every occasion that position was offered to you. I felt as if you were doing that only to spite me.'

Krishna's eyebrows almost touched his hairline as they puckered up enquiringly. 'What is the connection between my not wanting to be king to my wanting to spite you? And why would I want to spite you?'

'If you were king, my father would have become your friend and offered my hand to you—if only to improve his own standing with you. That way, I would have become your wife long ago, possibly even before Rukmini.'

Krishna laughed. 'Quite the contrary. If I was king, and your father had offered you in marriage to improve his own social status through this alliance, I would have refused to marry you. I am set against marriages of convenience. I am also opposed to girls being used as pawns in political games. This practice is so prevalent that it is accepted as if it is normal. But I believe a man and woman should unite only for love. For me, mutual trust is paramount for people entering the grihastashrama.'

'But then, why did you refuse to be king? What is the reason? That is an offer no one in their right senses would reject!'

'No Bhama! Neither power nor position add to one's character. I firmly believe that I am born for a purpose. And I think that that purpose is establishment of dharma, not in one place, but across Aryavarta, across the world, across the universe. A crown, I felt, would be a hindrance in the path as it would limit me geographically. I would lose my freedom of action while dealing with kings and kingdoms.'

Satyabhama felt bewildered. She shook her head and looked at him: 'But I always thought that power—political power—is necessary for achieving any major objective! And you, who wants to establish dharma across the universe, think that political power is an obstacle; that you can do it without political power...'

'Bhama, it is not my intention to downgrade the importance of political power. It can be used as a tool to engineer positive changes in human behaviour. But for that to happen, the person wielding the political power should be an upholder of dharma, recognize and respect it. However, I believe that dharma cannot be established through political power and weapons alone. Laws and wars can end lives physically. But only dharma and love can vanquish anger and hatred, which are the bane of human life on earth.'

Satyabhama felt elevated somehow. It was as if a burden had fallen off her shoulders. 'I have heard people say that you are God; are you?'

'Anyone who understands who he is, what he is, is God. God is sarvantaryami—one who resides in every being. Unfortunately, we, human beings allow our life, knowledge and skills become our identity—our ego. This ego overshadows all our perceptions and then we can see only differences; we lose the ability to see the same life force in every living being. Let go of the ego, make yourself the centre of your being, and then you can control the circumstances around you.

'Do you remember what happened at Govardhana Giri? Indra had caused a deluge as punishment for giving up a yagna to appease him. There was imminent danger for the entire Yadava race, along with all their livestock drowning in the flood.'

'Yes, I remember. I was there too. You lifted the Govardhana hill and held it like an umbrella over all our heads for an entire week! You could not have done that if you are not God!'

'I told myself that the same God resides in me as has created this wondrous mountain and each leaf and flower on it. So, for the sarvantaryami, there is no difference between me and the mountain. That means I am the same as the mountain. Lifting it up should be as easy as lifting myself. The hill that had nourished us and our cattle for generations with its fruit and water, would not want us dead for no good reason. That's all. I could pick up and hold the Govardhana Giri without any trouble. Indra got tired of his attempt at punishing us, but I was not tired. Indra called Varuna off after a week. He had realized his mistake.'

'Why did you oppose the Indrotsava? After all, that was an annual tradition followed by all Yadavas to propitiate Indra for bountiful rains? The event did protect us from the vagaries of nature. The first time we gave it up was the time when we faced Indra's wrath. So, why are you against yagnas and other worship rituals?'

'No, dear! I am not against worship. Nor am I against rituals. I only do not like it when the ritual is based on the fear of punishment, like Indrotsava was. The Yadavas worshipped Indra out of fear for his power to order Varuna to cause or cease rains. They believed that performing this elaborate yagna with rich offerings, would make Indra provide adequate rains as a reward. I believe that, any task or ritual undertaken or performed with fear as its basis or reward as a consequence cannot yield positive results. Any perceived benefits of such actions are only temporary. People who persist with them for a long time, would lose their vitality and initiative. Worship should be an expression of happiness—of gratitude for what we have, what we got from nature.'

Satyabhama was dumbstruck. Could she ever really understand Krishna! In the last few weeks since their marriage, he had never spoken to her on any serious issue like he did just now. While she knew that he was a unique person desirous of doing the right thing by everybody, she had not even imagined that he would be so profound. She felt very small in front of this idealist and she felt a sudden longing to change so as to be a befitting wife to him.

'Can I ask you something…' she started, only to see him stand up and stretch. 'No, you cannot ask me anything more. We are newlyweds. We have other things to occupy our time than indulge in philosophical debates. I want you with me in a different way. It is already late. Let us go in and get some sleep,' he said with a twinkle in his eye and pulled her up.

16

Mitravinda managed to haul herself up over the side of the boat, her long, frilly robes dripping. She was shivering, partly due to the intensely cold river waters, but largely with anger. She could guess that she had been left behind on purpose because her parents and brothers wanted to discuss her marriage. She was determined to not let that happen.

Raja Jayasena was the first to recover from shock with a surprised exclamation. 'What…how…what…,' he spluttered, unable to form a cogent question. Her twin brothers, Vinda and Anuvinda, were furious. They would have pushed her back into the waters, had their mother not come over with a blanket to wrap her daughter in. And, she, Rani Rajadhidevi was worried as to the repercussions of the development for her and her daughter.

'Why did you come?' Vinda thundered.

'Because I know what you are up to and will not let you get away with it,' Mitravinda's voice was firm in its resolve, despite the trembling caused due to the cold. She looked from one brother to the other and then at her father. 'What sin have I committed that you treat me like this, worse than your worst enemy?'

'That is a very unkind thing to say to your own father, Mitra. All of us are keen to find a suitable person for you to marry and lead a happy family life,' Raja Jayasena said, hoping that he would be able to douse his daughter's ire.

'Then why do it behind my back? Don't think I do not know why all of you came to the middle of the river; only to keep your decisions secret from me,' she looked accusingly at her two brothers and then included her father and mother as well.

'You are young. You do not know what is good for you. You do not even understand that we are trying to give you the best life possible,' Anuvinda said in a voice calculated to stop all further argument.

'It is my life. Should I not have a say in the matter?'

'Of course, my little one! There will be a swayamvara and you will choose your husband from among the invited kings,' Jayasena tried to be convincing.

'I do not need a swayamvara. I have made my choice. I want to marry Bhavuka Krishna,' Mitravinda declared.

'How can you be so foolish, Mitra!' Anuvinda tried to control his temper and be reasonable. 'Here we are trying to find a great king for you, and you insist on marrying that cowherd. He is not a king, and he has three wives already.'

'I do not care how many wives he has. I want to be his wife. I want to share his life. I will be happy if I can lay my head at his feet.'

'And what do you know of this fellow that you profess such great love for him?' Anuvinda could not hide his sarcasm, even as he put a restraining hand on Vinda who had lost his patience and was ready to get physically violent with their younger sister. Vinda shook his head and turned the boat around. The purpose of their trip had been defeated.

'How many times have you seen him, Mitra? Not more than once or twice! That is not enough for you to decide that you have undying love for him,' Jayasena's put-on patience was wearing thin.

Only Rajadhidevi sat there without saying a word, her eyes downcast. She just held her daughter close. The reason for her silence was that she knew that her word would carry no weight with either her husband or her sons.

Mitravinda looked disdainfully at her father, turned to her mother and then looked back at Jayasena. 'You can live a lifetime with someone and still not develop bonds of love and trust. Or you can just look at someone and recognize him or her as one's life partner; one's soul-mate.

'As to the number of times I saw Bhavuka, Pitashree, I am sure that I do not have to tell you that it is enough to feel one grain to know whether the rice is cooked or not. There is no need to touch every grain of rice.

'I will still answer your question—I saw Bhavuka only once— at his marriage with Rukmini. But I have heard about him—his actions and thoughts—through wandering singers when they passed through. I realized then that I could be happy only if I was close to him. In fact, mentally, I became his wife that very day. I submitted my life to him. The marriage has to happen only for the world to recognize me as his wife,' she stood her ground in the face of mounting anger in her brothers. She addressed them now, 'I know why you brought Matashree here like this. You wanted to pressurize her to agree to your plans, and then use her to pressurize me. You chose this place, in the middle of the river, only to ensure that I did not get to know about the meeting. But I did and came to fight my battle with you.'

They had returned, and Vinda and Anuvinda anchored the boat and walked off in a huff, without even the customary leave-taking from their parents.

'You are very unkind to me and your brothers, dear. We love you. You are my only daughter, and their only sister. It is our desire that you marry a great emperor, be an empress, a Maharani, wielding great power and someone whose reputation reaches every village in Aryavarta. Your brothers have been striving to improve their clout in Aryavarta so that they can take you to such a position.

'We came for a boat ride to prevent gossip amongst the servants in the palace, which can be detrimental to our plans,' Jayasena had come to sit by Mitravinda and was running a soothing hand over her head. He stole a sidelong glance at her and continued, 'Rest assured, Mitra, that nothing will be done against your wishes. We have a tradition of swayamvara for princesses to choose their husbands. You will select the groom yourself.'

Mitravinda felt a little confused. And cold. She was shivering in her wet clothes. She sneezed, a sure sign of an oncoming cold.

Rajadhidevi spoke for the first time since her daughter surprised them on the boat. It was possible that she felt slightly more emboldened to speak. '*Nath*, please let her get out of these wet clothes and drink something hot. Otherwise she will fall sick. We can talk later,' she said and hustled Mitravinda away.

In the security of Mitravinda's private chambers, she spoke again, even as she helped Mitravinda remove her wet clothing. 'Mitthu, I know you dream of Krishna and want to marry him. Nothing would please me better. That would renew my bonds with my parental family.'

Mitra nodded vigorously, glad that she had her mother's support. 'Yes, Mother. This is our tradition. A woman returns her own daughter to her parental home as a gesture of gratitude. In your family, although you are five sisters, you are the only one who has a daughter. So, it is your bounden duty to give me in marriage to a son of your brother,' she said forcefully, shaking her mother by the shoulder as if to remind her of her duty.

'No dear, you are not the only bhratvaja of Krishna. Don't you remember my sister Shrutakeerti, the Maharani of Kekaya? She has a daughter. Her name is Bhadra.'

'Oh!' Mitravinda dropped to the ground in a heap of disappointment. Rajadhidevi sat down by her, and putting a comforting hand around her shoulder, said, 'In fact, Shrutakeerti performed very rigorous austerities to get a daughter who would make an ideal wife for Krishna. While I have not seen Bhadra, I have heard that she is extremely beautiful and virtuous.

'Kekaya Naresh Drishtaketu has a formidable reputation as a righteous king. He has been a steadfast supporter of Krishna and the Pandavas. Your father and brothers, on the other hand, do not like Krishna. So, if Krishna is to marry a cousin, I feel he is more likely to select Bhadra than you.' There was hopelessness in Rajadhidevi's voice.

Mitravinda straightened up and looked directly into her mother's eyes: 'No, Ma. I do not know Bhadra, and I do not care whether Krishna weds her or not. All I want—and I am determined—is that I become a wife to Krishna.'

After a while, when Mitravinda spoke again, it was clear that some plan of action was taking shape in her mind. 'What is the reason for such deep hatred for Krishna in our family?'

Rajadhidevi was candid in her response. 'Actually, your father has no enmity towards either Krishna or the Pandavas. It is Vinda and Anuvinda, who are set against your Bhavuka. You see, all three were disciples of Acharya Sandipani. I heard that Krishna was very popular among their fellow-disciples. Your brothers found that unpalatable—Krishna, a cowherd, was admired more than themselves, princes. Also, Krishna turned out to be a much better archer than them. Yet another reason, I think, is what happened at Gomantaka Giri.'

'What happened at Gomantaka Giri, Maa? I do not seem to have any recollection of this,' Mitravinda's curiosity was piqued.

'Vinda and Anuvinda were a part of the confederation of kings

led by Magadha Sarvabhowma Jarasandha to Gomantaka Giri.
Jarasandha mounted an offensive to kill Krishna to avenge the death
of his Jamata Kamsa. Krishna was then a young boy of fifteen or
sixteen and lacked the wherewithal to face the combined might
of this group. Had he stayed on in Mathura, the entire Janapada
would have been wiped out. So, to save Mathura and its people,
Krishna and Balarama fled from there.

'Mathura was saved, but Jarasandha learnt that they were
sheltering at Gomantaka Giri and led his huge army there to
finish Krishna. But as things turned out, it was Krishna who saved
Jarasandha from a fatal blow by Balarama and spared Vinda and
Anuvinda's lives too. That is a humiliation your brothers have not
forgotten and have extended it to the Pandavas also.

'It is for this reason that they want to forge closer ties with the
King of Hastinapura, Kuru prince Duryodhana. Giving you to him
in marriage is a part of that same strategy,' Rajadhidevi concluded.

Mitravinda boiled over with rage. 'I knew it! And Pitashree
does not tire of talking about a swayamvara, where I will be free
to select whom I like! Where is the freedom?'

'Please do not be harsh on your father or brothers, Mitthu. They
have their compulsions. Running a kingdom is not only tough, but
also involves sacrifices and adjustments. And it is not as if they are
throwing you to the wolves. They do have your happiness at heart.
Duryodhana is a very nice person and desirable as a life partner
in many respects. He has a streak of vindictiveness in his actions,
but that is because of his peculiar circumstances.

'Mitthu, remember that it is not always possible for anyone,
and particularly a woman, to do what pleases her. A woman has to
put her personal preferences second to the larger family and the
national interests,' Rajadhidevi said.

'My wanting to marry Krishna is not detrimental to either

our family interests or the welfare of the Avanti Kingdom. I will not let anyone sacrifice my happiness for their prejudices. Also, I completely support Krishna Bhavuka's principled stand that princesses should not be used as pawns for a perceived political advantage,' Mitravinda said and turned to leave the room.

She stopped at the door for a moment, and declared, 'I am not an expendable pawn; I will not be a pawn. I know how to protect my self-respect.'*

---

*In another version, Krishna and his elder brother Balarama are described to be intentionally not invited for the svayamvara. Balarama was upset that they had been excluded for the marriage of their cousin Mitravinda. Balarama had also conveyed to Krishna that the svayamvara was a ruse as Vinda and Anuvinda wished to marry their sister to Duryodhana of the Kuru Empire. The marriage would forge alliance between Kuru and Avanti and also garner the support of Vidarbha and Magadha Kingdoms, which make the Kauravas very powerful. Balarama told his younger brother to abduct Mitravinda as she loved Krishna. As Krishna was not sure of the love of Mitravinda, he took his younger sister Subhadra along with him to quietly ascertain the wish of Mirtravinda. After Subhadra confirmed Mitravinda's love for Krishna, Krishna and Balarama stormed the svayamvara venue and abducted Mitravinda, defeating the princes of Avanti, Duryodhana and other suitors.

Krishna and Arjuna collapsed near a clump of trees, laughing and completely out of breath. The two cousins, who were more friends than relatives, were enjoying their time together, racing along the banks of River Yamuna.

Krishna was visiting Indraprastha, the new capital from where Yudhishtira was administering the Kuru Kingdom as its 'Sarvabhowma', its emperor. This in itself was a cataclysmic development, wherein Krishna had to employ all of his diplomatic skills to ensure that the Pandavas were not cheated once again and banished to the woods.

A similar thought crossed Arjuna's mind. 'But for your intervention, we would have been nowhere, Bhavuka.'

'I am but an instrument in the hands of the sarvantaryami. Everything happens for a purpose and everything happens at the right time, even though we are unable to appreciate it when seemingly negative things happen to us,' Krishna said, thinking back to that eventful day after Draupadi swayamvara in Kampilya.

The congregation of kings and other eminent personalities from all over Aryavarta were witness to the Pandavas revealing themselves to be alive and not dead, as had been presumed for over a year then. Arjuna had won the archery contest and Draupadi's hand. All the five brothers had married the Panchala princess in deference to their mother's wishes.

Bhishma and Vidura, under guidance from Veda Vyasa, decided that Yudhishtira, who had been the crown prince till he was presumed dead in the accident, should now be made the emperor. Duryodhana, who took Yudhishtira's place as the crown prince and thus expected to be crowned emperor, lost his chance.

Yudhishtira was crowned Sarvabhowma at an elaborate nine-day ceremony, making him the rightful heir to his grandfather Shantanu's crown and throne. These had been locked away reverentially by Pandu, who became king instead of his elder brother Dhritarashtra on account of his blindness. Towards the conclusion of the Vedic ceremony, Dhritarashtra surprised everyone by announcing that he wanted to delineate the areas to be governed by his sons and his deceased brother's sons. The assembled gathering was stunned when he declared that the Pandavas would rule from Khandavaprastha and his own sons would continue to reign from Hastinapura. Khandavaprastha lay on the outskirts of the Kuru Kingdom along the banks of Yamuna.

Krishna was at his charming best when he thanked Dhritarashtra for his foresight in partitioning the land. 'Your desire that Yudhishtira should work to restoring the prestige of the ancient Kuru dynasty is evident in assigning this old capital city, from where Emperor Shantanu ruled. The decision is truly great and praiseworthy. Yudhishtira will move to Khandavaprastha with all the symbols of "Chakravarti Sarvabhowma". And Duryodhana will rule Hastinapura as a regent king under the emperor. Oh, judicious king! I hope I am reading the meaning of your declaration right,' he had said, leaving Dhritarashtra with no option but to agree.

Krishna had gone on to list all assets of the kingdom to be shared by Dhritarashtra's sons and nephews, incorporating the compensation the Pandavas needed to make the shift and build a new city in place of the ruins of the old capital.

Dhritarashtra found himself in a tough situation, where he could not deny the assets being claimed by Krishna on behalf of the Pandavas but still unable to concede them. An amused Bhishma Pitamaha intervened and enthusiastically granted all that was sought. As a parting shot, Krishna had extended an open invitation to the general public, saying those who desired to be ruled by Yudhishtira could move to Khandavaprastha. They would be given all assistance to settle in the new place by the Pandavas, and Duryodhana, the King of Hastina, would grant adequate compensation for the immovable assets they would have to leave behind.

'We were able to build Indraprastha and settle there largely on account of the physical and moral support you provided, Bhavuka. Otherwise, we would have been living anonymously in dense forests, like we did before you produced us before the world,' Arjuna said with gratitude.

Krishna laughed it off. 'There is no place for formal thanks between friends and cousins. But you will be well advised to maintain a close vigil on developments in Hastina. Your Pitruvya and Duryodhana can only wish the worst for you.'

'You know, Bhavuka, ever since moving to Indraprastha (new name given to Khandavaprastha), life has been even and peaceful. It is so nice to see Mother comfortable and well looked after. All through our growing years, she had a hard time. Now, the thought of welcoming a grandson into the family has made her really very happy. She takes special care of Subhadra due to her pregnancy.'

Krishna recalled the circumstances under which Arjuna had married his little sister Subhadra. Arjuna was at the fag end of his year-long pilgrimage, taken up as punishment for having intruded the privacy of Yudhishtira and Draupadi. At the time of their polyandrous marriage, they had drawn up a code of conduct for themselves vis-a-vis their shared wife. It was decided that Draupadi would spend one year with each brother, and none of the other brothers should intrude into their private quarters. Breaking this rule would be punishable with an year-long pilgrimage to all the sacred rivers as atonement for the transgression. On one occasion, when Draupadi was with Yudhishtira, Arjuna was forced to enter their private chamber for his bow to deal with thieves, who had stolen a brahmin's cow.

It was a dicey situation. On one side was their sacred agreement of conduct and on the other was the survival of a cow and calf. The cow was stolen—possibly to be butchered, and the calf faced certain death from starvation and separation from its mother. Arjuna decided that he would rather take his punishment than let a cow and calf, also the brahmin's family, suffer.

He succeeded in intercepting the thieves and recovering the stolen cow and Arjuna's action came up for examination. All the brothers agreed that Arjuna had a valid and pressing reason for his action and so be condoned. Arjuna disagreed. It was a question of their credibility among the people, he said.

'Arjuna, you are a lucky fellow! Even a punishment turns into an advantage for you,' Krishna laughed with unbridled mirth. 'You acquired three wives and had two sons during that single year,' Arjuna joined in the laughter.

'Two of those marriages had a degree of compulsion to them. I had to oblige the *icchadhari nagakanya* Uluchi because she took a fancy to me while I was bathing in the Ganga and carried me down into Naga Loka. She gave birth to our son, Iravata, by the time I resurfaced in the river by dawn the next day.

'I met Chitrangada while I was a guest with King Chitravahana of Manipura, which was the last stop on my pilgrimage route. I was quite taken in by the princess's beauty. She reciprocated my feelings, and the king offered to conduct our wedding, if I was agreeable to one condition. The condition was that I would not be allowed to take my wife with me. She is the next in the line of succession to rule Manipura and her son would become the king after her. I agreed. We were married and a son, named Babhruvahana, was born to us.

'Leaving Chitrangada and Babhruvahana was tough. I miss them even now. But it was time for me to move on and I started on my way back. Then, I remembered that you had promised me a gift. I decided to visit you and collect my gift from you,' Arjuna laughed.

'I lived up to my promise and engineered your wedding with my younger sister Subhadra. We had to engage in a bit of subterfuge to keep Bhaiya Balarama in the dark till the wedding was over,' Krishna said. 'You know that Bhaiya is very fond of Duryodhana. He trained Duryodhana in mace fight, and ever since, Bhaiya wants to make him happy in any way he can. He bemoaned Duryodhana's bad luck when he wasn't crowned the emperor of Hastina and thought that giving our sister Subhadra as bride to him would somehow compensate for this loss. But I was keen that Subhadra marries her love, and I knew she had set her heart on you.'

The two cousins, who were now brothers-in-law, continued their light-hearted banter thus. Dusk was falling when Krishna suddenly decided to go for a swim. Krishna's short sentence declaring his intent took Arjuna by surprise. But Krishna had sprinted into the waters even before Arjuna could ask questions. Arjuna followed his wife's brother into the dark waters of the Yamuna.

Krishna swam very fast, changing direction often. Arjuna had a tough time trying to keep pace with him. It seemed as if Krishna was searching for something in the waters. When Krishna finally came out of the water, Arjuna followed him. Arjuna felt that there was a reason for Krishna's action, but did not want to ask prying questions. He waited patiently.

'Partha, I see a lady standing on the shore, all alone. Will you please go and find out who she is, and what she wants.'

Arjuna turned and looked towards the river. It was quite dark by now and he could hardly see anything, what with the undulating waves of the river throwing a mesmerizing mix of light and shadow. This, coupled with leaves swaying in the mild breeze, made it difficult to make out any form clearly. What did Krishna see? Arjuna looked towards the river, and then back at Krishna before purposefully striding towards the river. He walked up and down a couple of times before he spotted the lone figure. Arjuna thought his eyes were playing tricks on him. She seemed to emerge right from the middle of the river. Was she floating on the waters? Arjuna was not sure.

'May I know who you are and what you are doing here all alone at this time of the day? Is there anything that I can do to help you?' he asked. Despite the gathering darkness, Arjuna could see that she was young and extremely beautiful in a very unconventional way.

'Oh, sir, your kindness is truly heart warming, I am gratified by your offer of help.

'I am the daughter of Surya Deva. I am an ayonija. My name is Kalindi. Since taking on this body, I have wanted to have Krishna as my husband. I have practised severe austerities to achieve my objective. My father created a living space for me in the waters of this river. He said Krishna has a great affinity with this river and that he would definitely come here one day. I have been waiting here for long, and since this is my home, I consider Yamuna as my mother.

'My father told me that Govinda is an avatar of Shri Mahavishnu, and that he will accept me as his wife. A while ago, when I was meditating on him, I felt his presence in these waters. I came out in the hope of setting eyes on him.'

Kalindi's voice as she introduced herself felt like a thousand veenas making music. Arjuna was lost in a trance at this brush with divinity in its purest form. He collected his thoughts and introduced himself to her. 'You were right about Krishna's presence in the waters of the Yamuna. He is here. I am his cousin and my name is Arjuna. I will go and send him to you. Please wait,' he said and hurried back to Krishna.

'You are a fine fellow, Bhavuka, sitting here like this when you knew what is happening. You knew about Kalindi even before you sent me there to her, didn't you?'

'Hey Arjuna! Easy with your accusations! How was I to know who that girl is. Tell me, who is she and what does she want?'

'She says her name is Kalindi; she is Surya Deva's daughter. She has been meditating on you since she was born, in these river waters, waiting for you to come and marry her.'

'Partha, I knew that this was to happen. Bonds forged in the last birth are coming to claim renewal from us now. In fact, the relationship we share in this birth also has its base in our previous births. We make bonds of different kinds with different people during a lifetime. These come back to claim our affection in our later births.

'Don't you see, Partha! I have occupied the minds and hearts of different people in different ways. Ma Devaki, *Aatya* Kunti, *Anuja* Subhadra, Rukmini, Jambavati and Satyabhama…they all love me in their own different ways. Kalindi is yet another one, whose love for me is of yet another kind. It is like the brightness of Surya Deva reflected in different ways in waters of different places. The sarvantaryami also reflects differently in different people. Are we not here to fulfil the aspirations of those that seek us out?'

Arjuna was confused. He did not know if it was his Bhavuka in front of him or the *Jagatkaraka Vaasudeva*! His words were profound. In one moment, they clarified everything in an instant. At the very next, he felt stupefied, unable to understand a single word that he had heard.

Krishna walked over to him and placed a friendly arm over his shoulder. 'Arjuna, the Yamuna is my friend, my companion. She had a role in saving my life. She made way and enabled my father Vasudeva to walk through her. I spent my childhood on these banks. The river shaped my life. I feel that I know every wave in this river intimately, every grain of sand on these banks is a confidant. Now, Yamuna is gifting a damsel to me. Is it not my bounden duty to accept her?'

He patted Arjuna on the shoulder and took his first step to meet his future wife.

18

It was early morning. The very first rays of the rising sun appeared to be lovingly caressing the earth after the long dark night. The dewdrops on leaf tips and the ends of grass blades broke into rainbow-like colours, welcoming the day with a smile.

'The Sun will bless your son to be as great as he is,' Krishna said and squeezed his sister Subhadra's hand affectionately. The brother and sister were walking barefoot on the carpet of lush green grass of Subhadra's private garden in Indraprastha. Subhadra smiled bashfully at her brother's reference to her delicate condition.

Kalindi, Krishna's fourth and latest wife, sat on an ornate bench placed tastefully near a flowering bush. She was looking intently at the rising sun. 'She is so serene and contented,' Subhadra said as the duo passed by and wondered why she did not want to walk with them.

'She is talking to her father, that's why,' Krishna replied. 'She is a *tapasvin* and is totally untouched by this world. She does not need human interactions, as average human beings do,' he added.

'Yes, I noticed and that made me wonder why she wanted to marry you, or why you agreed to the proposal,' Subhadra looked questioningly at her brother. She almost lost her balance as she stubbed her toe against a small stone half hidden in the grass. Krishna instinctively tightened his grip on her hand, using his other hand to steady her.

'Careful!' he admonished and spoke after a thoughtful silence. 'It is difficult to explain human relations. A lot depends upon the people we met and dealt with in our last births. I think she is here to augment my strength in the mission I have set myself in this life.'

'I would have thought that Rukmini Vadhunika was enough for that. She compliments you perfectly and she had supported you fully in all the three years before you brought Jambavati Vadhunika home. She seemed very lost in the initial days, and would have probably remained that way, but for Rukmini Vadhunika's support and guidance. Your next wife, Satyabhama Devi! Who would have thought that you would agree to marry that hot head!'

'Hey, little one! Mind how you talk about your elders. She is also your Vadhunika.' The words notwithstanding, there was a hint of a smile in Krishna's voice.

Subhadra caught it and chuckled. 'I know I can speak my mind with you, unlike with *Peddanna*. I meant no disrespect. I was only comparing their personalities. They are beautiful in their own different ways. Rukmini Vadhunika has grown up in regal surroundings, is a skilled diplomat with good understanding of politics, and she made you go to her with her love and commitment. Jambavati Vadhunika is unworldly! She is untouched by anything called intrigue or selfishness. She is pure and must have imbibed reverence to Srihari from her father. And she treats you like God.'

Krishna gave a light tap on his sister's shoulder. 'Is that all? My wise little Subhadra has not given her comments on her youngest vadhunika—why?'

'Wisdom is not your private preserve, *Chinnanna*. I am a grown-up and know how to assess people. And I will tell you what Satyabhama Vadhunika is like. I admire her very much. She is spirited, knows what she wants and strives to get it. She can set aside propriety and social niceties that become obstacles in her way. The only troubling point with her is her stress on wealth.

'Actually, you and Rukmini Vadhunika make a perfect pair. When you did not marry for almost three years after she came into our family, and given your preoccupation with all that is happening around us, I thought you would not marry again.'

'That is enough personality analysis for one morning. And enough walking for you! The sun is getting hot, we must go indoors,' he said and led her to where Kalindi was sitting. She was still gazing at the sun—the brightness of the sun's rays did not seem to bother her.

'Shall we go in, Kalindi?' There was immense compassion in Krishna's voice as he extended a hand to this ethereal beauty.

Kalindi turned her lotus-shaped eyes to her husband, nodded and smiled as she took his hand, and rose. Kalindi rarely spoke. Her eyes answered all questions.

Even as the three were walking back, Krishna with his sister on one side and his bride on the other, a messenger came with news that there was a visitor for Krishna.

'Swetaketu,' Krishna called out in sheer joy when he met his caller in the hall and hugged him in welcome. 'How did you know that I was here? Are you well? How is Acharya Sandipani? What brings you here…' Krishna showered enquiries on his friend. Swetaketu was Acharya Sandipani's principal disciple and had trained several of the Acharya's students. He was now managing the ashram as the aging Acharya had gone into semi-retirement.

'I come here from Ujjaini bearing a message for you from your Aatya Rajadhidevi.'

'I hope you bring good tidings, Swetaketu. I heard that Swasruva Jayasena has not been in good health of late.'

'Your information is correct, Krishna. Maharaja Jayasena's health has suffered a setback. He has retired and now, the elder of the twins, Vinda, is the king, and Anuvinda helps him in administration. Unfortunately, both brothers lack the sagacity needed to take the kingdom forward. It is sad to see a janapada like Avanti, which has immense potential to rise as a frontline state, unable to push ahead due to weak leadership. I do what I can by way of tendering advice, but the brothers still flounder.

'That is sad. Avanti, under their father had developed as a centre of great learning, and despite pressure from Jarasandha of Magadha, he had held his own. Now, there is a qualitative change in the political situation in the region. Jarasandha has stopped meddling with other janapadas, after Draupadi's swayamvara and her subsequent marriage with the Pandavas. That was an opportunity for assertive action to catapult Avanti into a frontline state.'

'Unfortunately, the two brothers feel insecure with the growing popularity of Indraprastha under Yudhishtira. They firmly believe that Duryodhana has been wronged. They see him as a capable leader dogged by bad luck.' Swetaketu gave a wan smile and continued. 'They hold you partly responsible for Duryodhana's plight. They think that you have cleverly cheated him out of his due and had a major chunk of the kingdom's assets transferred to the Pandavas.

'They are, of course, free to think what they want. But trouble is that they are worried that Avanti would lose itself under the expansionist plans of Indraprastha. They refuse to see that Indraprastha has not occupied any sovereign land, possibly because of their own sense of insecurity. So, to counter this perceived threat from Yudhishtira, they want to join forces with Duryodhana.'

Krishna said, 'Their perceived threat from Indraprastha does not change anything on the ground. In any case, friendly relations between Avanti and Hastinapura are welcome. What makes you worry, Swetaketu?'

'The reason for my worry is that their idea of improving relations and increasing their combined clout is through marrying their sister Mitravinda to Duryodhana. They are organizing a swayamvara for her and they are trying to influence Mitravinda into choosing Duryodhana as her husband. This is the reason that brought me to you. Queen Rajadhidevi and Mitravinda are both opposed to this proposal. They want you to come and intervene.

'I tried to dissuade them, because the swayamvara is scheduled for next week, and King Vinda has expressly ordered that you are not to be invited. He thinks you can spoil things for him.'

'And how does Queen Rajadhidevi think I can help?'

'It is Princess Mitravinda who offers a solution. The proposal is fully endorsed by her mother.'

Krishna waited.

Swetaketu took a deep breath and continued, 'Mitravinda professes deep love for you and urges you with folded hands to abduct her from the swayamvara sabha and marry her, like you married Rukmini.'

Krishna did not respond immediately. He closed his eyes. Swetaketu knew he was in deep thought and waited.

'Swetaketu, I do not have to state that my sympathies are with my Bhratvaja Mitravinda. She should not be forced to marry anyone against her wish. Yet, she should not jump into another matrimony as an escape. Her desire to avoid one problem should not lead her into another. You say that she does not want to be married to Duryodhana. Since a swayamvara has been scheduled for her, she should select someone she loves among the invitees.

'I intervened in Rukmini's case, because I knew of her affection for me and responded to her appeal because I reciprocate her feelings. I knew Rukmini's feelings for me for about five years before our marriage. Aatya Rajadhidevi is possibly keen to uphold the prevalent custom of gifting a daughter to her parental home through a marriage to a bhavuka. Please tell her that I am honoured with her offer, but cannot accept it because I am not sure that this is what Mitravinda wants.'

'Gopala, please do not be harsh on Mitravinda. Acharya Sandipani has known her since she was a child. He has deep and abiding affection for her. He has inculcated the highest regard for dharma in her. In addition to hearing about your various missions and actions through wandering minstrels, she has followed your journey closely and developed respect and love for you. The Acharya is convinced of her love and commitment to you. He has asked me to tell you that he requests you to accept Mitravinda as your wife.'

Krishna remained doubtful and non-committal.

'I will also put my weight behind the Acharya and request you to take Mitravinda as your life partner. I too have seen her from close and know that she holds you as her swami.'

Krishna closed his eyes again, thinking. Swetaketu watched anxiously. He, like Acharya Sandipani, was keen to see Mitravinda as Krishna's wife.

Krishna's lips parted in a smile before his eyes opened. He slapped Swetaketu's shoulder and said, 'Let us go back together to Ujjayini, starting from here tomorrow. That way, we can reach by the day before the swayamvara. I will need to talk to Mitravinda and know for sure she wants to be my fifth wife. Only if I am convinced on this score will I take her. However, since I am not invited for the swayamvara, the option of her selecting me in public cannot happen.'

❧

It was a hot, lazy afternoon. Not a leaf moved and it felt as if air itself had stopped moving. Mitravinda felt lonely and lost. She came out into the courtyard to find a comfortable place under a shady tree to pass these hours of intense heat. She settled with her back resting against a shady tree. She closed her eyes and let her mind wander.

She had been in Indraprastha for about a week now, and had become Krishna's wife just a couple of days back. The marriage was solemnized at Indraprastha itself, as Krishna's family—parents Devaki–Vasudeva, elder brother and his wife Balarama–Revati—were all here. Kalindi's marriage to Krishna was also celebrated at Indraprastha just a couple of months ago.

Krishna's family had come from Dwaraka to visit Subhadra, who had eloped with Arjuna some months earlier. The elopement had happened under Krishna's guidance. He desired to avoid a confrontation with Balarama with regard to Subhadra's marriage. Balarama wanted his sister to marry his favourite disciple Duryodhana, but Krishna knew about her love for Arjuna. Balarama accepted the marriage without much protest and had joined his parents and brother on this trip to felicitate the newly-weds. Before setting out for the trip, Krishna had entrusted the administration of family affairs in Dwaraka to Rukmini. The last message from her, which had arrived on the very day of Mitravinda's wedding, contained nothing to worry about. She was able to manage very well. Nothing suffered because of the absence of the three men of the family. Satyabhama was helping her and even Jambavati was now being trained in managing family affairs.

Devaki and Vasudeva brought gifts and presents for the newly-weds and others in Arjuna's family. Arjuna's mother, Kunti Devi, was Vasudeva's sister and was extremely happy to see her brother and his wife after many years. She spent long hours with them, sharing her troubles from old times. She was widowed when her children were all still very young and had to live in Hastinapura under the protection of Dhritarashtra and Gandhari—no easy thing. Unburdening herself to her kith and kin was the catharsis she needed.

When it came to light that Subhadra was pregnant, Kunti urged Devaki and Vasudeva to stay on till the grandchild arrived. The request was gladly accepted, and news about the changed plans was sent to Dwaraka.

It had been an eventful trip for Devaki and Vasudeva. Their only daughter, born more than eight years after their eighth son, Krishna, was born, had not only got married, but was with child. It would be their first grandchild, for neither Balarama or Krishna had any children. Even for Kunti, this grandchild was precious, even though, technically, it was not her first grandchild. Bheema had got married to *rakshasa kanya* Hidimbi, soon after they escaped from Varnavata. A son, Ghatotkacha, was born of that marriage. Living in the jungle amidst man-eating *rakshasas*, Kunti was unable to appreciate the grandson then. When they left, they could not bring either Hidimbi or Ghatotkacha with them on account of the rule of the land in the Nagakoota jungles. Arjuna, during his one year of exile (for having intruded on Draupadi and Yudhishtira's privacy), had sired two sons—Iravata from *naga kanya* Uluchi, and

Babhruvahana from Chitrangada, the princess of Manipura—but Kunti had not seen either since they remained with their mothers in their respective kingdoms. Draupadi was as yet childless.

Mitravinda remembered her own eventful swayamvara. She was tense with worry when Acharya Swetaketu, who had carried her message to Krishna, did not return till just the day before the swayamvara. But he had conveyed good tidings to her mother, and she had eavesdropped from behind a curtain. Krishna would come to take her away; she would be saved from having to select Duryodhana. What happened on the day of the swayamvara was even more interesting, and she heard of each development from minute to minute.

Krishna was challenged by her brothers at the palace gates. They insulted Krishna, telling him that he had not been invited to the swayamvara because he was ineligible; he was not a king and only kings were invited to participate. Krishna acted surprised; said he was not aware of it; and anyway, he had not come for the swayamvara. He had brought his newly-married sister and brother-in-law for blessings from his aatya, Queen Rajadhidevi. They sought the queen's blessings for the child she was carrying in her womb, he had said.

Vinda and Anuvinda were in a dilemma. They could refuse entry to the suitor Krishna, but not to a jaameya, and definitely not when he was accompanied by a pregnant woman and her husband. In fact, the visitors had to be received with the full honours due to a family member. Mitravinda had enjoyed hearing descriptions of her brothers' predicament as they formally received the guests.

The guests were with Rani Rajadhidevi when the swayamvara commenced. Mitravinda was escorted along the rows of suitors. Anuvinda and Acharya Swetaketu walked with her on either side. They paused in front of each suitor and his particulars of family background and personal achievements were extolled. A couple of her sakhis walked beside her with a garland in an ornate plate. She could either take it and garland the particular suitor or just move on to the next.

At one particular moment, as if on cue, the acharya led her into the central aisle. Krishna was there—no one quite realized how or when he came. Mitravinda snatched the garland from her sakhi and threw it around his neck. By the time her brother Anuvinda had recovered enough to draw his sword, Krishna had led her by the wrist and jumped into a chariot standing right at the entrance. Arjuna was holding the reins and Subhadra helped her settle in her seat. The chariot galloped away, even as armed guards tried to mount an offensive.

Mitravinda smiled at the memory. What bliss! They had reached Indraprastha to a rousing welcome by the entire family. A priest was waiting to conduct the wedding.

The combined sounds of rustling clothes and tinkling laughter intruded into her reverie and Mitravinda opened her eyes. She found Kalindi, Subhadra and Draupadi standing around her, gurgling with laughter. She had not realized that she had slid down to a supine position with her hands locked under her head. She sat up in confusion, adjusting her garment to cover her bosom and her cheeks turned a burning pink.

'Daydreaming is not permitted,' Draupadi said in mock seriousness, shaking a finger at her.

'Sleepless nights do make you drowsy during the day,' Subhadra said with an elaborate show of understanding.

Kalindi said nothing, her expression one of divine serenity. She felt no regret at having lost the tag of 'new bride' to her husband's next wife, Mitravinda realized, and was filled with wonderment at Kalindi's lack of discomfort.

'What were you dreaming about, vadhunika?' Subhadra teased.

'We thought we would play paccheesi to take our minds away from this heat,' Draupadi said, shaking the small bag of shells she carried in her hand.

Kalindi smiled, more with her eyes than with her lips.

Mitravinda allowed herself to be pulled up by Draupadi and all four women went in to sit around a table with the paccheesi board spread on it.

Initially, conversation centred on the game as it was completely new to Kalindi. She proved to be a quick learner and very soon she was playing it as well as anyone else. Slowly but surely, the game itself became secondary and conversation turned to personal experiences. All of them came from different backgrounds and there was much to share and learn.

Subhadra spoke of her early years. She had grown up thinking she was her parents' only child. She was about seven years old when she met her two brothers. Devaki taught her to call them 'Peddanna' and 'Chinnanna'. And slowly, as time passed and she grew older, she learned that her parents had lost six sons due to their Mamaka Kamsa's cruelty; that they spent all that time in a prison because of a prophecy that Kamsa would be killed by Devaki's eighth son. Subhadra talked about her mother's firm belief that Peddanna and Chinnanna were 'God', or at least specially blessed by God, since they escaped death at their Mamaka's hands. Her parents had gone on a pilgrimage for more than six years to prevent their anxiety for their sons' safety from exposing them. 'I was born after they returned and settled in Mathura. For me, Peddanna and Chinnanna are gods. I feel so loved, so cared for and so secure in their presence,' she said.

Mitravinda spoke glowingly about her mother Rajadhidevi. She had had an isolated childhood, as her father and brothers believed that women should be kept subservient. Possibly her two brothers did not consider women as equals and her father, on account of his excessive love for them, adopted a similar attitude towards women. Her mother was not allowed to visit her brother Vasudeva in Mathura because he was not a king, and so, lacked status.

Krishna's escapades formed the staple diet of stories she heard on her mother's lap. As she grew up, she understood the deeper meaning of those stories when she heard them from wandering minstrels. She remembered a day, she was about seven or eight, when she had declared her eternal, undying love for Krishna and her determination to marry him when she grew up. Her mother had hugged her and wept saying she lacked the freedom to practice the well-established tradition of giving her daughter to a brother as '*jami*'. That was a turning point in her life. She had wiped her mother's tears and taken an oath that she would certainly become Krishna's wife. She repeated this promise everyday to herself from then on and would have committed suicide rather than be somebody else's wife, she said.

Kalindi put an understanding arm around Mitravinda's shoulders. She said she too had lived her life just wanting to be Krishna's wife. She was lucky that her father Surya Deva, who put the idea of Krishna into her mind, had left her in the care of River Yamuna to wait for Krishna. 'Krishna loves this river. He has played in these waters, and you will understand Krishna well if you live in these very waters,' he had told her.

By now, the paccheesi board lay abandoned and conversation took up the women's full attention. Unlike her usual reserved demeanour, Kalindi contributed liberally with interesting and little known details about the Yamuna. The river was her mother and her home, she said, and talked about how she communicated with her father. By contrast, Draupadi maintained a studied silence. It took a lot of prodding from Subhadra and Mitravinda to make her open up. However, when she did speak, she surprised the others with her frankness.

'The Draupadi you see in front of you is a very different person from what I was when I was young and growing up.

'Like Kalindi, I am an ayonija, not born of a womb. My father, the King of Panchala, took the unusual path of yagna to get children. The reason why he wanted children was to be avenged. He was steeped in hatred and vengeance when he did the yagna and we—my brother Drishtadyumna and I—were instruments gifted by Agni Deva for his revenge. I was determined that this body given by my father must be used to achieve his purpose. I trained alongside my brother in all the martial arts.

'As time passed, we realized that we could not achieve our objective through our own strength; that we would need help. My father learned that Krishna was the best archer among Acharya Sandipani's disciples—comparable to Arjuna, the best of Drona's students—and offered me in marriage to him.

Krishna did not want to marry me as that would lead to enmity with Arjuna, his best friend and dear cousin. He had another and a stronger objection to the proposal. It would be against a principle he holds dear—using marriage as a tool for political purpose, and more importantly, it would increase the sapping negative emotions that my father and Drona Acharya nurtured in their bosoms for so long. He told me that he would help me get the best archer as my husband if that was what I wanted, and in the process cleanse us of the debilitating negativity of hatred. He managed that; he restored the old bonds of love and affection between my father and Drona,' Draupadi looked dreamily into the distance, a sigh of relief escaping her, as if it had just happened.

'But there was another problem immediately after your swayamvara. There was so much discussion about that,' Mitravinda recalled what she had heard about the polyandrous marriage.

Draupadi smiled. 'Yes, that was a tricky situation; Swasruva Kunti Devi wanted her five sons to share the bounty won by one son. She offered to retract, but the brothers insisted that her word was a command. Thanks once again to Bhrata, it was resolved.'

'How did he convince you?' Subhadra asked.

'You see, the issue was about one girl marrying more than one man. This hardly ever happens. Generally, it is one man marrying many women. *Pujya* Gurudev Veda Vyasa, who was called in to explain points of principle and dharma, said this was an extraordinary situation which called for an extraordinary solution. Polyandry was not against *sanatana* dharma and he cited instances where one woman married several men.

'Then he explained that marriage as an institution was devised to protect humanity from the ill-effects of all-consuming passion. Animals do not need any rules because their passion is seasonal. Since humans do not have this limitation, setting rules for this indulgence was considered necessary as safeguard against excessive sexual desires. The requirement is for both men and women to remain steadfast in their commitment to one person at one time. So, a woman who does not want to become *sati* with her deceased husband can marry again and honour *pativrata* dharma. If it is a child that a woman desires after her husband's death, she can have it through either her husband's brothers, or through a learned Brahmin. And, when a woman marries more than one man, the rule is that she show the same commitment to them all.

'Then *Bhrata* Krishna put forth the options I had in my particular case. He said that it was for me and me alone to make my decision.

'Since it was Arjuna who had actually won the swayamvara, I would be quite right in insisting that I marry him alone. In that case, Arjuna himself would feel guilty at going against his mother's word, and the burden of being separated from his brothers would weigh him down. He would be an unhappy person.

'Alternatively, since this was not a situation that I had asked for or created, and I was being asked to marry five brothers, I could reject the result of the swayamvara. In such an event, my father, whose stature had risen significantly because of the manner in which the swayamvara was conducted, would lose face and prestige. He would be guilty of not delivering on his promise of getting his daughter married to the winner of the swayamvara. It would harm the Pandavas also, as they would have to stand up to Duryodhana without the support of the mighty Panchala, and the challenge could be tough for the Pandavas. And I would be back to square one, where I started. I would have no husband despite the successful completion of the swayamvara and my chances of selecting a husband would stand compromised.

'The third option was what Yudhishtira had suggested—marry them all. That would give the brothers the satisfaction of having honoured their mother's word; there would be unity in the family, and with the assured support of Drupada Maharaja, the Pandavas could take on Duryodhana and his supporters. With a Swasruva like Kunti Devi and five brothers united in their commitment to dharma, I would be surrounded by dharma.

'The choice was mine,' Krishna said, 'and you all know what I opted for,' Draupadi concluded with a laugh, and looked at the others, who joined in her laughter.

❧

20

Mitravinda was packing her few personal belongings. She was humming softly, an indication that she was happy. Happy to be heading home. Mitravinda smiled to herself as she realized that the word 'home' now stood for Dwaraka and not Ujjaini. Not that she had not been happy at Indraprastha—she had received a whole-hearted welcome when she had first come here a couple of months ago. She had bonded with Subhadra almost instantaneously when they met in Ujjaini, and by the time they set foot in Indraprastha, they felt deeply attached.

Arjuna instinctively donned the role of an elder brother to her, protecting her from Avanti's soldiers as they tried to prevent their princess's abduction from the swayamvara sabha. *Matrushya Kunti Devi* was like her own mother. She resembled her sister physically and showered unconditional affection on her. Devaki and Revati were open and supportive of her. Draupadi and Kalindi too accepted her as a family member. Draupadi, particularly, went out of her way to make her feel welcome and ensured that she did not lack anything she needed for a comfortable stay. She had exerted herself similarly for Kalindi also. Even so, Mitravinda felt homesick. She had left her parental home, but had not reached her destination, her home in Dwaraka.

They had stayed on to welcome Subhadra's child into this world. Since it was almost a month after Subhadra had delivered her son, named Abhimanyu, they should be on their way, Mitra had suggested to Krishna. He had agreed and had gone to take his leave of Arjuna and Subhadra.

She heard a sound—it was Krishna, she thought, and turned to the door, wondering who he was talking to. It was Arjuna, coming to persuade her to extend their stay. His argument was that they should await Abhimanyu's younger brother, currently growing in Draupadi's womb. 'Draupadi is as much a sister to Krishna as Subhadra is,' he pointed out.

Mitravinda could not disagree, but said that they could all come back when the baby arrived. Arjuna did not press further, but settled for an easy chat. Conversation moved from subject to subject and veered round to his favourite subject, Krishna's childhood deeds.

'*Govinda*, I heard that you had tamed a wild *vrishabha* when you were just seven. Is this true?'

Krishna laughed at the memory. 'It is true. This ox was a terror. His name was Hasti and all the kids would run for their lives when they heard it approaching. One day when all of us were talking about it, Bhaiya said there was no one who could tame this wild and aggressive vrishabha. I said I could, and we decided I would attempt this on the next full moon night.'

Mitravinda did not want to miss the chance of hearing her husband relate one of his many miraculous deeds that she had only heard of as stories told and retold, getting embellished in the process. She settled down to listen.

'I used the intervening month to get friendly with it. I would go every night and play my murali near its enclosure. Gradually, the music had an impact and the vrishabha mellowed down. After a while, it accepted jaggery and green grass from my hand. Music became a bridge of communication between us and it would wait for the notes of murali.

'This wager was kept secret from all the adults. All the boys collected on the banks of Yamuna to see what would happen. I said I was ready to ride on the ox and asked if any of the boys wanted to join me. None did. But Radha came. Her confidence was she could come to no harm if I was with her.

'The vrishabha walked serenely to me, completely at peace with everything around him and bent his head to be patted. I climbed on its back. Radha sat behind me and the vrishabha ran. Bhaiya got worried for me and ran to inform Bapu and Mahee,' Krishna laughed softly, his eyes dreamily shut, and back in his childhood.

'Do you still think that wild animals respond to music?' Arjuna asked.

'Yes,' Krishna was certain.

'Even if there is more than one such animal?' Arjuna persisted.

Krishna straightened up and looked into Arjuna's eyes. 'You have something on your mind. Say it.'

'Kosala Mahajanapada is said to be facing a similar problem. Here, there are seven vrishabhas. They are all very ferocious and behave as a team. They charge at anyone who tries to approach them. Do you think you can tame them?' Arjuna's eyes challenged Krishna.

'Of course I can,' Krishna was all cool confidence.

'But now you do not have your murali to make music with. Shall I get one for you now?' Arjuna was still teasing Krishna.

'Partha, tell me this. How does sound originate?'

'Through movement in air waves.'

'Right! There is constant movement of air in human bodies. Death happens when this movement ceases. These air waves produce a constant sound, which is called "*omkar*" or "*anahata*". Beings whose sense organs are fine tuned are aware of this sound and derive a kind of blissful happiness from it. Flutists use these very airwaves to magnify such sounds, which we call "music" and spread happiness.

'Beings with such acute senses also have the capacity to spread these sound waves around them without the help of any instrument or implement. They can use these waves to influence others. If the receiving person has similar acute senses, he can even recognize them as they enter his body. If it is someone who lacks this developed sensibility, he may not be able to recognize what is happening, but will surely be influenced by them. So, not having a murali with me now is not going to be a hurdle.'

'Bhavuka, are you sure that animals also respond similarly to soundwaves?'

'Yes. They have no conscious understanding of what is happening, but do get influenced,' Krishna said as he looked closely at Arjuna. 'I know there is some ulterior purpose for your questions. So come, spell it out.'

'The King of Kosala, Nagnajit, has a daughter named Nagnajiti. Some time ago, he had announced that he would give his daughter in marriage only to a person who can tame all the seven vrishabhas simultaneously. Given Nagnajiti's reputation as an unparalleled beauty, there was no dearth of courageous kings and commoners who tried their luck. All of them have failed, because these beasts behave as a team and charge at any intruder who tries to touch any one of them,' Partha said, looking closely at Krishna for a hint of fear or hesitation.

'Oh! That makes it even more interesting,' Krishna said, slapping Arjuna's back enthusiastically.

'Bhavuka, I am amazed at your enthusiasm. You have five wives already, yet you are ready to try your luck for another!'

'Arjuna, I know you asked this question in jest. Even so, it has serious connotations and I would like to answer it truthfully.

I have no interest in gaining a reputation for the number of wives I have. Nor am I driven by sexual urges that seek variety. Quite a few souls have taken birth as women to serve me through a marital relationship. I have to oblige them and keep the promise I made to them in my previous avatar.'

Mitravinda felt lost. She was unable to tell whether she was awake or dreaming. Arjuna's question had a vital significance for her and she had perked up her ears to hear Krishna's answer. While Krishna was sitting right in front of her, his visage had acquired an aura of surrealism. He seemed to be very far removed from the confines of her room. His voice had a booming quality, which at the same time, seemed whispered into her ear.

She was jolted into the present by the laughter-filled voice of her husband, shaking Arjuna by the shoulder. 'Hey Partha! Where are you lost! You were saying something about aggressive vrishabhas…'

Arjuna shook his head vigorously as if trying to clear it. 'I really do not know what happened. Yes, yes… I was telling you about these vrishabhas in Kosala. Would you like to try your hand at taming them?'

'Yes. But only if this queen will grant me permission,' Krishna was back to his usual playful self. His eyes danced mischievously as he walked up to where Mitravinda was sitting. He folded his arms across his chest, bent forward to his waist in mock humility and asked, 'Devi, do I have your permission?'

'Of course! You must go and return victorious! I have grown up listening to stories of your brave deeds. Now, as your dharma*patni*, I am blessed to be a part of one such extraordinary deed. All I desire from life is the good fortune to be by your side at all times.'

'There you are,' Krishna spread his hands out as he turned to Arjuna. 'Tell me, when are we to start?'

'I will finalize the programme in consultation with our priest. I will ask him to give us an auspicious time.'

Krishna smiled. 'Partha, remember this. A thought for action arises in one's mind only when there is a divine design. The timing is a part of this cosmic jigsaw. So commencing an action when the thought strikes is honouring this cosmic law, acknowledging the power of the supreme being. Acting in good faith and to the best of our ability is our duty. Trying to find an auspicious time is interfering with nature's scheme of things and denotes an ego that questions the sarvantaryami. So setting out right away would be the right thing to do.'

'Bhavuka, you confuse me. I do not know what to think. I have no objection to leaving right away if you are ready... But I will need a little time to organize a chariot with strong horses, a few men who can accompany us on this trip and take care of necessities along the way,' he said and added as he hurried out, 'I shall make the arrangements right away.'

Copious tears were rolling down her cheeks. Mitravinda was either unaware of her tears or had tired of all attempts to stop them. Her thoughts were elsewhere. She was trying to understand her own self; her feelings.

Why was she upset? After all, she had bid farewell to her husband willingly. She had told him that she was not a narrow-minded woman who took offence to her husband taking another wife. After all, she herself had entered Krishna's life as his fifth wife. She was content with her status as one of Krishna's wives. Kalindi, whom Krishna married barely a few weeks before her, had welcomed her.

'But then, Kalindi is not quite normal—she had no contact with anyone on earth; all she ever did was bide her time in the waters of Yamuna, waiting to be taken by Krishna. So her reaction to a new co-wife can hardly be taken as "normal, human behaviour",' Mitravinda countered herself.

'What about Vahni Rukmini?' The question echoed from the dark hollows of her large bedchamber. Rukmini had sent gifts and a welcome message though a messenger from Dwaraka, as soon as she had heard of her wedding with Krishna. She could not dismiss them as a formality, devoid of meaning or any real warmth, for she knew that Rukmini had received both Jambavati and Satyabhama with open arms, and had helped them settle down in their new environs.

No! She was not selfish; she was not grudging the entry of another wife in her husband's life. It was actually the fact that, for the first time in her life, she was away from her parents. While she was mentally prepared to move to a new home with her husband when she married, she was still en route even after nearly an year. Her journey had paused at Indraprastha.

As long as Krishna was around, time just flew! Even though the Pandava family exerted itself to make her feel welcome and at home, it was Krishna's presence that mattered. His absence made life seem pointless. Her bedchamber, where she had spent such happy hours in the loving arms of Krishna, now had a barren feel to it. It was an eerie silence.

Krishna had left with Arjuna early that morning and she filled her time with the others. She had accompanied Draupadi on her walk, spent time with Matrushya Kunti talking about olden times, played with little Abhimanyu and chatted with Subhadra and Kalindi. Now it was night and she had to return to her private chambers. She had walked around the room and even ventured out into the sitting room where Krishna often received visitors. Krishna's absence struck her the harder for it. Then she tried lying down with her eyes tightly shut, hoping sleep would claim her senses and thus help her cope with her loneliness.

But sleep eluded her. Imagination tormented her. Why did Krishna want to marry so many times? Is it because the wives he had were unable to satisfy him? Would there ever be an end to the additions to the number of his wives? Did that mean that the women he had married till now –Rukmini, Jambavati, Satyabhama, Kalindi and herself—suffered from certain inadequacies?

And then there was Radha! He had mentioned her yesterday when Arjuna spoke about the vrishabha Hasti's taming. She could feel his ecstasy when he uttered that name. There had always been much speculation around Radha. According to some stories she had heard since her childhood, he had married this girl, who was much older than him, when he himself was still a child. Other stories said she was his first love, and that he held her memory very dear.

What was she to do when Krishna walked in with another wife? Welcome her and watch helplessly as he frolicked with her?

Tears flowed from her eyes. She tried to divert her thoughts and not cry. She had to be strong! But no! The tears would not stop. The more she wiped them away, the more freely they flowed.

Mitravinda sat up. She tried deep breathing to calm her nerves. The tears continued to flow. She just sat there, feeling miserable.

She was jolted into the present by a sound. Did she really hear it, or had she imagined it? Was it a knock on her door? She did not know. Then she heard it again. There was no mistake. There was somebody outside her bedchamber. Who could that be at this late hour! She really did not want to show herself to anybody just now. Her tear-stained swollen eyes would be a sure giveaway. But she could not ignore the knock any longer. The sound had become insistent now. She rose to open the door.

Krishna! It was Krishna standing there! She stood there, stunned. Had he not gone? Or had he turned back midway? Krishna put an arm around her shoulders and walked her back into the room. He closed the door and sat in a comfortable chair by the bed. He was smiling, and Mitravinda walked after him and collapsed at his feet, placing her forehead on his knee and hugging his legs with both her hands, tears still flowing from her eyes.

'So, this is my brave wife! She sees me off with a show of great confidence and then cries herself silly,' he teased her as he stroked her head.

Mitravinda flushed at this reference to her weakness. And his touch on her head made her tingle all over. Making an effort to keep her voice even, she asked, 'What happened? Has your journey been cancelled for some reason? Has everyone returned with you?'

'No, Mitra. The journey is on. We stopped for the night. I felt your sadness and came to be with you. I started on this journey only after you gave me permission. I asked you more than once if you were agreeable to my going. You should have been frank and said no. I would not have gone at all,' Krishna pulled her up into his lap and wiped her face with his *angavastra*.

He put a finger under her chin, forcing her to look him in the eye. 'Mitra, remember that you have married me to be happy. Not to shed tears. Be assured that your Krishna will never do anything to hurt or displease you.'

Mitravinda's spirits rose. He cared; he cared for her; he cared for her more than his other wives! He cares for me the most! These thoughts made her very happy. 'Swami, have you given up the trip?' she asked, barely concealing her relief.

'No, beloved! The journey is on as planned.'

'Then…how are you here?' She felt confused.

'Yes. I am here. What could I do? I could not see you crying.'

'Now you are fooling me. How did you know I was crying? No one knows! And you want me to believe that you, who were so far away, saw my tears!'

'Devi, why do you think like an uneducated, ignorant person? Do you not remember what the acharya taught you—a husband and wife are one soul with two bodies. So you are within me at all times. Then how can I not know your grief?'

Mitravinda's eyes widened in disbelief. 'Then…then…what about my other vahnis in Dwaraka?'

'Have no doubt. They do not miss me. They are also within me. I am not away from them either.'

Mitravinda tried to digest this information. 'How about my

brother Arjuna? Does he know that you have returned?'

'No. Because I am travelling with him.'

Mitravinda shook herself, but the confusion refused to clear. 'You mean you are here and there also?' she asked.

Krishna's voice was full of softness, love and understanding. 'Yes, Mitra. I am here. I am there. I am everywhere. In fact, there is no place where I am not present. You wanted me here with you, so I am here in the form that you desired.'

'You have more than one form?' Mitravinda's eyes widened in surprise.

'No, my dear! It is the same form. But until you realize that there is no difference between you and me, our physical forms will keep us separate.'

Mitravinda looked around. She and Krishna were no longer in the confines of her bedchamber. They were in an endless vast expanse filled with a mysterious light in which nothing was clearly visible. Krishna's form filled her. She felt herself merging into him. Her perspective changed. Now, she could not tell whether the words she heard through her entire being were emanating from Krishna or from herself.

'This form is necessary till there is the universal realization that I exist in all beings. Till then, there is a need for Krishna and Mitravinda to have physical forms, marry, have children. When every being feels this oneness with me, I would have achieved the purpose of this *avatar*. I would then have served the purpose of dharma. You, Rukmini, Radha, Kalindi, Kunti and the Pandavas, Acharya Sandipani, Swetaketu and so many others have appeared in this world to help me in this task.

'All these people have different roles in different places, with different tasks to perform, and different objectives to achieve. I am there in all of them, guiding them along their paths. Some of these people have identifiable relationships with me as parent, sibling, wife, friend and so on, and there are so many others who are my devotees. I am connected with everyone and am there for them when they need me.'

Mitravinda was jolted back into reality. She looked around and found herself where she was—in her bedchamber. She remembered that Krishna was to have been with Arjuna *en route* to Ayodhya. She was being selfish in detaining Krishna here with her.

'Prabhu! You should return to *Bhrata* Arjuna. You have a task to achieve. This task would suffer if you are here and your form alone is there.'

Krishna smiled again. 'There is no difference between me and my form because the essence in both is the same, just like every single drop of water in the river is the same as the water in a container.'

Mitravinda felt at peace with herself. She perceived Krishna as all pervasive. He was within her. He filled her. She was in him. She closed her eyes; she dozed off. When she opened her eyes again, she was in her bed. Krishna was gone.

Krishna peeped through a small aperture in the 20-feet-high iron gates of the enclosure that housed the seven vrishabhas. He could not see anything. He adjusted of vision to get a clear view of another part of the huge enclosure. He saw one of the vrishabhas. Its skin was a shining indigo blue-black, and it looked more like a mountain than an ox.

That was enough for Krishna to realize that this was no normal vrishabha. It was not just its size, which was daunting in itself. The largest bull he had seen was Hasti in Vrindavan, which responded to music. Hasti would be like an ant in front of an elephant if it were to be brought before this vrishabha.

Was it possible that the vrishabha felt his presence? For, it turned towards the gate. The next moment there were sounds like thunder from within the enclosure and Krishna saw the remaining six vrishabhas surround the first one. The sight was chilling. Krishna counted, trying to identify each vrishabha separately and understand each one's specific characteristics. It was not possible given the limited view he had through the little hole.

A wave of anticipation ran through Krishna. His experience as a Gopala stood refreshed and ready for use. He stepped aside and nodded at the King, indicating that he was ready to face the vrishabhas. The Maharaja, who had seen many a valiant young man mauled and gored to death by the vrishabhas, hesitated and asked,

'Are you sure you want to do this?'

Krishna had already tied his dhoti tight around his waist and thighs. 'Yes,' he said firmly, leaving the king with no option but to order his commander to open the gates.

Krishna had to bend double to pass through the opening in the gate. He had seven ropes to yoke the vrishabhas, which he slung casually across his shoulder. Once inside, he straightened and looked calmly at the seven vrishabhas as they gazed at him. He knew that he could not even consider dealing with them one by one. All seven had to be approached simultaneously.

Krishna breathed deep, took up seven identical forms and in a trice, was amidst the vrishabhas. He jumped high and held each ox by its horns, using the elbow of his right hand to deal a forceful blow right in the middle of its eyes. Before the oxen recovered enough to attack him, Krishna had thrown the ropes around their necks and knotted each one tight enough to prevent any of the beasts from escaping, yet taking care that the knots were loose enough to allow them to breathe. The task achieved, Krishna once again merged into one body, held all seven ropes in his right hand and led them to the gate.

Nagnajit could not believe his good fortune when he heard Krishna call out for the door to be opened. 'The small hole will not be enough. Please have the gate opened wide for me and the vrishabhas,' he said.

Nagnajit had his eye glued to the same hole after Krishna had entered the enclosure. He could see Krishna's back as he took small, almost imperceptible steps forward. He could make out the outline of the seven vrishabhas as they stood as one huge mountain sizing up the intruder.

Suddenly, Nagnajit felt that his eyes were playing tricks with him. He saw Krishna's back expand and split into multiple bodies.

By the time the king rubbed his eyes and looked again, he could not see anything. It was all a blur of dust. Even as Nagnajit was trying to peer through the haze, apprehensive of seeing the young man's mauled body in the dust, he heard Krishna's voice asking for the doors to be opened.

The King was overjoyed to see Krishna come out without a scratch on his body. He was holding the yoked vrishabhas by their ropes in one hand and readjusting his dhoti with the other to let it fall to his ankles. Then Nagnajit did something that was strictly prohibited in royal etiquette. He stepped forward and embraced Krishna, felt his cheeks and shoulders for further reassurance that he was really in front of him, and kissed him on the crown of his head.

He ordered his commander to take charge of the vrishabhas and hold grand celebrations across the kingdom.

Word was sent to Nagnajiti and she came out, accompanied by a couple of her intimate sakhis who helped her place a garland around Krishna's neck. The couple was married the very next day.

That evening, Krishna and Arjuna accompanied Nagnajiti to the terrace of the royal palace to enjoy the scenic beauty of the city. It was a pleasant evening with a mild breeze blowing from the distant Himalayas. The terrace of the imposing palace was so high that it seemed possible to touch the sky just by raising a hand. Arjuna rose and walked around, more to provide some privacy to the newly-weds than to look at anything in particular. Nagnajiti sat quietly with lowered eyes, playing with the bangles on her hands. 'You seem to be in serious thought. Are you wondering how you will manage with your co-wives, now that you married a man with five wives?' Krishna asked.

Nagnajiti's lips parted in a smile. She looked Krishna straight in the eye and shook her head.

Krishna raised his eyebrows in question.

'I am married to a man who yoked seven ferocious vrishabhas. How can I be worried about dealing with my husband's five other wives?'

'You and your father both hold these *sapta* (seven) vrishabhas in very high esteem. King Nagnajit made great arrangements to safeguard them, when he could have just left them in the wild to fend for themselves. Having cared for them for several years and knowing that they were beyond human control and could never be domesticated, he made taming them a precondition for your marriage. I wonder why.' Krishna tried to read an answer in his new wife's eyes.

'They are very special and have been kept in my father's custody. I will need to explain this in some detail for you to understand. Do you really want to know?'

Nagnajiti continued after Krishna nodded. 'These are not vrishabhas by birth. They are the creation of the *sapta-rishis*. The stellar rishis, being human, were a combination of the *satvik*, rajas and *tamo guna*s. Because of their highly evolved consciousness, these *rishis* were not only aware of these three types of gunas in them, but were able to separate them with their *tapas-shakti*. They then combined all their purest *satvik guna*s into a flower to be presented to Shree Mahavishnu and combined their rajas and tamo gunas to form these seven vrishabhas. They knew that only Mahavishnu could overpower them.'

'I see! And what has happened to that flower of purity so painstakingly shaped by the *maharshis*?' Krishna queried with a smile.

'It has been offered at the feet of Shree Mahavishnu,' Nagnajiti said.

Krishna bent forward, putting his face very close to that of

Nagnajiti, forcing her to look into his eyes. As their eyes met, it seemed as if the rest of the world around them had dissolved into nothingness. 'Nagnajiti, I recognize you as the combined positive power of the sapta-rishis, placed in my care for use in the task of reforming the world on the path of dharma. You are a gift to me by the sapta-rishis, and I cannot be grateful enough to them for it.'

The spell was broken by the return of Arjuna wanting to know the name of a river he spotted to one side of the palace. Krishna evinced keen interest in seeing the river and Nagnajiti walked with the two cousins to point to river Gomati.

Nagnajiti proceeded to point to various other structures of importance around Shravasti, Kosala's capital. She then pointed a finger in the general direction of Ayodhya and Saketa. She said these two cities were highly developed and were comparable to Shravasti in every aspect. 'In fact, there is an astrologer among the palace priests who suggested shifting the capital to Ayodhya. The change in the seat of governance, he felt, would brighten the chances of finding the right husband for me,' she laughed, referring to the tough task her father had set for her marriage.

Nagnajiti pointed further afield to neighbouring Videha and the towering Himalayas in the background. For no apparent reason, Krishna became alert. He shielded his eyes with one hand and focussed on a flying bird-like creature in the distance.

He left Naganjiti and Arjuna to admire the beauty of the Himalayas and moved away from them to the other end of the terrace. Both Nagnajiti and Arjuna noticed an ethereal being alight in front of Krishna and the two engage in earnest conversation. The two shifted their attention back to worldly attractions, acknowledging Krishna's need for privacy to deal with the ethereal being.

That evening, the bridal couple was escorted along the major thoroughfares of Shravasti with celebratory fireworks and music by renowned instrumentalists. The entire city had been lit up and decorated for the occasion. Gaily dressed people lined the streets to throw flowers at the princess and her husband. This was followed by a royal feast at which special invitees blessed the newly-wed couple and showered them with gifts.

It was much later that night, when all the guests had departed that Krishna and Nagnajiti were left alone. In fact, this was the first time that the two were alone together, barring those few moments on the terrace when Arjuna was present in the background. 'Prabhu, I notice that something is weighing on your mind. Would you like to share it with me and unburden yourself?' Nagnajiti asked with a trace of hesitation in her voice while helping Krishna remove the crown from his head and setting his *angavastra* on a nearby shelf.

Krishna smiled. It was an intimate smile that put Nagnajiti completely at ease with her new husband. She sat next to him on the soft bed and looked into his eyes. 'I have no secrets from you, Nagnajiti. And if I ever come up against a problem, I know I can depend upon your judgement to resolve it in the most dharmic manner,' he said, reaching out to hold her hand in his own.

Krishna took a moment to organise his thoughts. Nagnajiti waited. 'You must have noticed that a lady came to meet me on the terrace.' Nagnajiti nodded. 'She arrived from the sky. It shows that she is a person with divine powers,' She responded.

'Yes, she is Shruti Ranjani, an expert in *shodasha kala* the sixteen arts. She has been deputed to train Bhadra Devi, my Bhratvaja from Aatya Shrutakeerti and Swashruva Drishtaketu, the Queen and King of Kekaya Kingdom.'

Nagnajiti waited for more. But Krishna remained lost in thought. 'Did she bring a message for you from Aatya Shrutakeerti and Swashruva Drishtaketu?' she asked.

Krishna snapped out of his thoughts and gave one of his mischievous smiles. 'She brought a message alright, but you are wrong about the source. The message was from Bhadra Devi,' he said and watched his new wife closely for a reaction. There was none beyond a mild curiosity.

'Bhadra Devi has sent me a personal invitation for her swayamvara.'

'You are beyond comparison, Bhavuka! You set out to tame oxen and return with not one, but two wives,' Bhima said, slapping Krishna on his back, and laughing uproariously.

His four brothers—Yudhishtira, Arjuna, Nakula and Sahadeva—joined the good-natured ribbing of their friend, guide and philosopher cousin, Krishna Vaasudeva. The women of the family were comfortably seated around the central courtyard of the matriarch Kunti Devi's personal palace, and were enjoying the fun being poked at Krishna. Kunti, who understood the strong bonds of love and affection between her sons and her jameya, was sharing their laughter, even as she was protective about the new entrants into the family. She did not want them to be excessively embarrassed. Kunti also kept an eye on Draupadi, who was pregnant with her first child from Yudhishtira. She cradled little Abhimanyu in her arms, and cautioned against loud laughter, particularly by Bhima—it could disturb the sleeping child.

'He is a *veera-putra*, Mother! He is not one to get perturbed by mere sounds,' Bhima countered.

The boy's mother, Subhadra, meanwhile, was very much a party to the ongoing fun made of her Chinnanna Krishna and added her own bit to the laughter.

Nagnajiti and Bhadra Devi, the latest additions to Krishna's family of wives, blushed at the jokes and jibes at Krishna because he had married them both with less than a week in between. They tried to hide behind pillars. Kalindi and Mitravinda, who had also become Krishna's wives in recent months, tried to conceal their giggles behind their pallus held across their faces.

These kind of gatherings were rare in royal families anywhere in Aryavarta. Palace protocol decreed that women were not to be seen at all, unless there was a specific need for it. They were called upon to serve a meal on occasions when there was a royal guest. They would then be dressed and bejewelled so as to underline the king's standing and the guest's importance. Their faces would be covered with a veil, with only their hands visible. All their interactions with their husbands, sons, brothers and fathers happened within their private living quarters. But Krishna opposed such segregation as discriminatory. Families should spend time together—only then would bonds of love and affection be nurtured, he maintained.

The Pandavas and their mother Kunti Devi adapted to these open sessions without any difficulty. Their years in the jungle had taught them to be flexible in their attitude. For Krishna, Arjuna's wife Subhadra was his *bhagini* and he had accepted Pandava Patni Draupadi as his *bhagini* as well, when he first met her and offered to help in selecting a suitable husband for her. Among Krishna's four wives, Mitravinda and Bhadra Devi were *bhagineyi* to Kunti and so, like her own daughters. She accepted Kalindi and Nagnajiti as sisters to her bhagineyi and therefore like her own nieces. By extension, Krishna's wives had the status of sisters to the Pandavas.

Arjuna lent his support to Bhima. 'Bhrata, you can well imagine my situation. I was right there, not knowing what to do! I tried my level best to rein him in. I told him that it would be seen as unseemly haste to plan his next wedding with Bhadra on the very day he was married to Nagnajiti! And I was the lucky man steering his chariot,' he said, raising another round of unbridled mirth.

Krishna, the butt of all the jokes, sat in bashful silence. His trademark mischievous smile in place as he stole frequent glances at one or the other of his wives.

Draupadi, who was sitting next to Yudhishtira, came to Krishna's rescue. 'It is unfair to say such things to Krishna *Anna*.'

Draupadi had started addressing Krishna as '*bhrata*' after her swayamvar, but had changed her address to the more intimate '*Anna*', just like Subhadra. Subhadra's entry into the family as Arjuna's wife made Krishna more of a brother to her, and her desire to be at par with Subhadra for Krishna's affections was at the root of this change in the form of address.

'It is not Krishna Anna's fault at all. What can he do if princesses send emissaries requesting him to come and marry them?' she argued. Krishna smiled thankfully at her and exchanged another naughty look with Bhadra.

'Yes, I was right by him when a lady landed on our terrace and pressed him to marry Bhadra,' Nagnajiti spoke ever so softly. Her words were meant only for Bhadra, who was next to her, and she put a friendly arm around her. The two new brides laughed softly and Kunti was happy to note the bonds of friendship blossoming between them. Draupadi also smiled at them, indicating that she shared their happiness.

Arjuna claimed credit once again. 'Bhavuka married four times within this past one year and I was by him on all four occasions. This makes me much more than a blood brother to his brides, and I promise that I will always be there for them.'

Everybody clapped in appreciation. Arjuna held up a hand, suggesting that he had not finished yet. 'And I have a promise to make to Bhavuka also. I assure him that I will extend all possible help, if he ever wants to marry any other girl in future,' he said in mock magnanimity.

While everyone laughed, Sahadeva cleared his throat. Sahadeva was a man of few words, and when he spoke, his words were heard in silence. Now too, everybody turned and waited for him to speak. 'I think Bhavuka does have something to ask of you, Bhrata.'

Attention now turned to Krishna. Kunti prodded him, 'My dear Krishna Vaasudeva, Kanha! You are very special to us. If there is anything at all that we can do to gladden you, to make you happy, be assured that no effort would be spared to have it done for you.'

Krishna looked around the room. His eyes danced with laughter. Yet there was a note of seriousness in his tone when he spoke. 'I am a much-married man. I married seven times in the last ten to twelve years. I should not be thinking of any more marriages for myself.' Krishna surveyed the room once again. 'Yet, I want to marry once more; I have an unfulfilled wish.'

'What is that wish, Krishna? Say it and my brothers and I will make it come true for you,' Yudhishtira promised.

'I either abducted my brides and married them or had them gifted to me. I never won a contest to win a wife,' he looked at Arjuna suggestively. Everybody fell silent, trying to understand what Krishna meant.

Arjuna nodded knowingly. 'I understand what you mean. You are an all-rounder—an excellent archer, and skilled in all martial arts—whether it is fighting with a mace, freestyle wrestling, or sword fighting, and you miss not demonstrating your skills in public. So, what we can do...' Arjuna stopped mid-sentence to look up at his youngest brother Nakula walk in with a scroll in his hand. Nakula had stepped out a while earlier when an attendant announced the arrival of a visitor.

'The visitor we just had was a messenger from the kingdom of Madra. He delivered this invitation for the princess of Madra, Lakshana's swayamvara. It says that the princess desires to select the best archer as her life partner. The winner would be selected on the basis of a contest to be held in the capital of Madra, Saagala, on the fifth day of the month of *Kartika*,' Nakula looked up from the scroll in his hand.

Laughter erupted in the room. Nakula, who had gone to meet the visitor and so did not know the conversation between Krishna and his brothers, looked surprised. There was nothing funny in what he had read out. It was a simple, straightforward invitation for a swayamvara. Why was everyone laughing?

Arjuna walked up to Krishna, pulled him up by the hand and slapped him on the back. 'Is it possible that our Bhavuka wishes for something and that does not magically happen immediately?' he asked no one in particular.

The invitation became the central point of discussion from then on. Yudhishtira declared that Krishna must participate in the swayamvara and have the satisfaction of exhibiting his archery skills.

'Yes, he must prove that his skills are not limited to abducting brides from their swayamvara sabhas,' Bhima laughed his throaty laugh that somehow filled the whole area.

'Yes, Bhavuka. We will all go with you as part of your delegation,' Arjuna said, only to be vetoed by his eldest brother Yudhishtira. 'There are urgent matters of governance that need attention here. You and Bhima go with him. I will manage here with Nakula and Sahadeva and make preparations to receive Krishna and his next vallabhi.'

❧

24

Krishna was pacing up and down the banks of the Yamuna, tormented by self-doubt. The river had been like a second home to him, almost like a mother. It had nourished him, rejuvenated him, given him solace and joy. Just looking at its serene waters brought calm to him, provided answers to questions, solutions to problems and enabled him to deal with tough choices. He often felt that the Yamuna spoke to him.

Today it was different. He had been here with the river for over an hour, but answers eluded him. He felt deprived. He, who prided himself on knowing the pitfalls of inflated egos and on keeping his own ego in check, was now hankering after another marriage; that too barely one week after bringing two new brides home. He would soon return to Dwaraka, there he had three more wives waiting for him. What would they say? How would they react to having to share him with his new wives? Was he being unfair to them? What made him marry so many women? Was he a flawed person; incomplete somehow?

No! Of course not! He married them because they wanted it. They were the ones who chose him as their husband. He only respected and honoured their desire. How could he be faulted for that?

He heard laughter. Was it the Yamuna? No, he realized that the laughter had come from within him. It was mocking laughter—

mocking him because he was justifying his multiple marriages on the grounds that he was responding to other's desire. In that case, how would he explain the swayamvara that he proposed to attend next week?

No, he had no excuse! Nothing to justify his stated desire to win in the archery contest in Saagala and marry Princess Lakshana! Should he opt out? Then he ran the risk of being seen as a coward, unsure of his prowess with the bow and arrow. Since he had already married seven women, would one more make a difference?

Krishna kicked hard into the sand in anger and frustration, lost his balance and sank into the soft sand. As he was picking himself up, he noticed some figures in the distance. He was surprised. This was a secluded stretch accessible only from the royal palace. Now the forms had come closer and he could distinguish four persons. From their clothing, it was clear that they were women. Then, he recognized them—they were his four wives.

He felt ashamed and contrite. He had come away without telling anyone. Now he was guilty of worrying them too. He did not feel like talking to anyone. Had he been on his feet, he could have walked away into the darkness without being seen. He did not know how to tender apologies for his action.

He was still trying to gather his thoughts when Kalindi, Mitravinda, Nagnajiti and Bhadra Devi reached him. They sat down by him. They reached out and placed a hand on his—Bhadra and Mitra on his right hand and Kalindi and Nagnajiti on his left hand. Krishna looked from one to the other in utter surprise and disbelief. Their touch had magically soothed him. The solace he had been trying to draw from river Yamuna without success, he got from his wives. None of them said a word. They just sat there, enhancing the serenity of the night.

'Are you all angry and upset that I hanker after a win at a

swayamvara contest?' Krishna asked, trying to read their expressions. The night was too dark for him to even guess their reaction.

'No, swami! This is another marriage that is waiting to happen.' It was Kalindi who spoke. Her voice, so rarely heard, was like music, like a thousand veenas strummed together. 'The princess of Madra is just like us. She too has grown up with a commitment to you. And you, Jagannatha, have a purpose in this life. You have to invite and accept each and everyone who wishes to be a part of you.'

'We are ready to welcome your new bride, who will be a sister to us,' Mitravinda said and Kalindi, Nagnajiti and Bhadra Devi nodded their agreement.

Mitravinda continued, 'I was ignorant in the past and worried about my future when you went to tame the vrishabhas and win Nagnajiti. I have shared my follies of that time with my co-sisters here. Now I have no apprehensions. I consider myself fortunate to associate with them.'

Krishna looked from one to another of his wives for any hint of doubt. He saw none. His eyes rested on Bhadra Devi.

A glowing smile lit up Bhadra's face. 'Nath! You are all-knowing. Did I not want to marry you, become your wife, knowing fully well that you already had six wives? Then, how can I object to your taking another wife, a wife of your choice?

'And moreover, it is quite common for men to marry many women,' she added after a moment.

'No, Bhadra! You are committing a grave mistake by comparing our husband with all other men. Our nath is 'Jagannath', husband to the entire world,' Nagnajiti said. She looked into the distance and she seemed to be talking to herself. 'We are the lucky flowers who have reached his feet in worship. Krishna is no ordinary mortal. He is here for a purpose.

'Yet, he too has to experience the fruits of previous actions.

When he donned a human form in the past, he had set an example for mankind, inspiring them to be faithful to one woman in one lifetime. Yet, he could not prevent women from yearning for his company, to become a part of him as *ardhanginis*. Shree Hari Jagannatha is here to satisfy this yearning. That is a part of the purpose of his appearance now.'

Krishna was mesmerized. Nagnajiti was no ordinary human being! Being the composite of the satvik aspect of the Sapta Rishis, she had insights that were beyond human capabilities.

Krishna was jolted back into the present by Bhadra's chirpy voice. She did not seem to have heard Nagnajiti's words.

'Becoming your wife was the major objective of my life for as long as I can remember. In fact, my mother prayed for a daughter that she could hand over to you as wife,' Bhadra looked around at her co-wives and continued, 'You see, my mother, Queen Shrutakeerti, is one of the five sisters of Yadava Mukhya Vasudeva. She felt sad that all the sisters only had male offsprings; not a single girl that could be returned to their parental home for the growth and spread of the family. So many other families continue to grow by this custom.'

'Hey Bhadra! You seem to have forgotten me. I am also a bhratvaja to Krishna. My mother, Queen of Avanti, Rajadhidevi, is also a sister to Mamaka Vasudeva,' Mitravinda interrupted.

'I have not forgotten you, Mitra. You were born to Matrushya Rajadhidevi only a few months before me. My mother did not know that you were on the way.

'When I was born, my parents were convinced that I came in response to their prayers. My father continued to pray for a competent guru for me so that I could be trained to be a worthy wife to Krishna. Guru Shruti Ranjani was the result of those prayers and she trained me in all sixteen arts.

'After vahnis Rukmini, Jambavati and Satyabhama became Krishna's wives, I became anxious that he may not even know of my existence and might never come to claim me. I pleaded with my guru and sent her to Dwaraka with a message of my love.

'The reply she came back with was encouraging, but there was no indication that he would act on my request. My anxiety surfaced once again after I heard of his marriages with you three, and persuaded Guru Shruti Ranjani to make another trip to *Bhavuka* while he was still in Shravasti.'

'Yes, I saw her. She has divine powers, I could see. You have imbibed all the best qualities from her, Bhadra,' said Nagnajiti.

Bhadra smiled in appreciation of the compliment and continued, 'There was more anxiety for me. My father organized a swayamvara for me because that is the tradition. He had not stipulated any condition because we knew whom I would choose. There would be trouble if Krishna did not grace the swayamvara. I shudder to think what would have happened if my prayers were not answered and Krishna had not come on time.'

'How could I disappoint you, Bhadra? I would have had to find a way out of it only if the offer of marriage had its roots in some political calculation. There was none. It was a sincere offer by an upright king. He nurtured you with such great care and brought you up to be a wonderful person. I am grateful to Swasura Drishtaketu for nurturing this beautiful flower for me, and enabling the smooth conduct of our marriage rituals,' Krishna said.

❧

All arrangements were in place in Saagala for Princess Lakshana's swayamvara the next day. The janapada was a lush green landscape—fruit-laden trees, flower-laden bushes and creepers imbued the air with intoxicating smells. The scenic beauty of this Himalayan kingdom competed with the colourful and extravagant arrangements made. Saagala wore a festive look for Raja Kumari Lakshana's swayamvara. A separate township was erected on the outskirts of the city to house the invitee kings and their delegations.

The swayamvara organized by King Brihatsena had attracted attention from far and wide. It was being compared to the swayamvara organized by the king of Panchala, Drupada, for his daughter about a decade ago. The reason was that the winner of an archery competition would win the hand of the princess here as well. Princess Lakshana's exceptional beauty was another reason why the royal community looked forward to it so eagerly. It was said that the princess had such fine *lakshanas* (qualities) at birth that she was named Lakshana. There was much speculation among the guests on who would be fortunate enough to wed her.

The presence of Magadha emperor Jarasandha gave rise to many a snide remark. Did this aging king still hanker for brides who were the same age as his grand-daughters? Or would he win the contest and claim the princess for his grandson Meghasandhi?

Some of the guests recalled that Jarasandha had gone for Draupadi's swayamvara; that there were rumours at that time about his plan to abduct her in revenge of Krishna's abducting the Vidarbha princess Rukmini from right under Jarasandha's nose.

Duryodhana, Raja of Hastinapura had arrived with a large delegation. He was seen as a regular at any swayamvara in Aryavarta, but with no conquests to show for it. His prowess with a bow and arrow was not questioned. He was also a powerful fighter with the mace, and also in freestyle wrestling. But for some inexplicable reason, he could not make the mark. He had to concede defeat to Bhima at the swayamvara of his wife Bhanumati's sister, Jalandhara Devi, even after it had been agreed between Duryodhana and his father-in-law that Jalandhara would join her elder sister in Hastina as his wife.

Vinda and Anuvinda, the king and *yuvaraja* of Avanti were there. So was Rukmi, the King of Vidarbha. They were considered lightweights with little chance of success at any competitive event.

The arrival of Krishna, accompanied by Bhima and Arjuna electrified Saagala, giving a fresh lease to ongoing speculation. Would Krishna participate? The general verdict was that it was unlikely, because he had always stayed away from competition. 'He is a sly person, who believes in abducting brides and marrying them,' many said and laughed derisively.

Arjuna was more likely to participate. He was a great archer—people still remembered how he had hit the target in the matsya-yantra set up at Kampilya. But that victory had led to a very unusual conclusion—Draupadi was made to marry all five Pandava brothers. Would it be the same this time too? Would Lakshana become another *pancha-bhartruka* like Panchali?

All the excitement died down in audible sighs of disappointment when the matsya-yantra that needed to be pierced was unveiled.

'It is by far the toughest such *yantra* set up anywhere', was the unanimous verdict among the guests and audience. The contestants were called upon to shoot a fish revolving in a frame above while looking at its reflection in the water below. This basic structure of the matsya-yantra was the same as the one set up in Kampilya for Draupadi's swayamvara. The change was that each contestant, who got five chances then, would get only two chances here in Saagala. The target fish, which rotated at varying speeds then, would rotate at varying heights now.

The rules of the contest were announced by the acharyas, who would also be judges. Each contestant was called upon to first string the bow and then shoot the arrow. No one was eligible for a third chance, it was stated.

Jarasandha was the first to move into the arena. He walked around the pond once, trying to gauge the chances of success, and touched the bow. He looked at the assembled guests once before complimenting the acharyas for the excellent *yantra* they had set up. Then, he turned to King Brihatsena and declared, 'I came not to participate but to be a part of the event and to bless Princess Lakshana.' He walked to where she was sitting, placed a hand over her head in blessing and walked back to his seat.

A hush fell over the assembly as Duryodhana rose to try his luck. On his way to the central arena, he had to pass a number of royal enclosures, and this included the enclosure reserved for the Pandavas. Even though he avoided looking in that direction, Duryodhana could not help noticing Krishna in the front row, flanked by Bhima and Arjuna. All three were engrossed in conversation, and just as he went past, he heard Bhima's laughter.

Duryodhana clenched his fists; Bhima's laughter never failed to rattle him. It had an irritating effect on him ever since they were small children playing and studying together. The sound irritated him now as well. It was like a bad omen, foretelling his failure. He remembered that he had heard this same laughter when he was trying to lift the bow at Draupadi's swayamvara. At that time, he did not know that the Pandavas were alive or that they were present at the same venue. Even so, his ears picked up and recognized Bhima's laughter. It had distracted and agitated him so much that he failed to knot the string at the other end of the bow. His big toe, which he used to press down the lower end of the bow, had slipped; he lost balance and fell!

And he was here in person! Why, oh why did he have to come, if not to ensure his defeat? More than the defeat, the insult it entailed. Duryodhana was unable to banish thoughts of his pet rival from his mind. This energy-sapping preoccupation impacted his concentration.

Duryodhana made a herculean effort to focus on the task at hand. He picked the bejewelled bow with his left hand and holding the bow string between the fingers of his right hand, managed to bend the bow and tie the knot. He pulled the string to check its tautness, and the resonating sound dulled Bhima's laughter in his ears. He knew that Bhima was not laughing just now, but its sound continued to ring in his ears and fill his mind.

Duryodhana walked majestically around the pond once before picking one arrow. He positioned himself at the edge of the pond, his left knee resting on the pond's rim and right foot balancing his weight. He lifted the bow with the arrow in position and looked into the pond. It was a blur. He could not see the fish, leave alone its eye. Either the fish was rotating too fast, or his eyes were playing tricks. He knew he could kneel there forever waiting for his eyes to adjust. He must release the arrow...release the arrow...release the arrow...

Duryodhana knew that he had missed even before the arrow left the bow. He did not want to try a second time. He walked back to his seat, a defeated man.

Duryodhana would have left the swayamvara pandal, but for the protocol of the event. All participants were expected to witness the proceedings from start to finish and congratulate the winner. The bride's father invariably invited all the guests to stay on till the wedding, and generally, most of them did. That was how he was forced to stay and watch Bhima marry his *syali* Jalandhara—when he had expected to be the groom himself.

When it was their turn, Bhima and Arjuna stood up and clapped loudly for Krishna Vaasudeva as he entered the arena. Krishna was at ease and a smile played on his lips. He looked towards the podium where King Drishtaketu and Princess Lakshana were seated. He caught Lakshana's eye and greeted her before picking up the bow. The next moment, the pandal was filled with applause for the winner. Krishna's arrow had pierced the fish.

Krishna was elated. He was happy like a child who had achieved a feat for the first time in his life. He put the bow back on its stand and hugged Bhima who had leaped over the barrier separating the arena from the seating enclosures. Bhima lifted Krishna up in his arms and pirouetted in joy. Arjuna reached them a moment later. The two brothers walked halfway up the podium to meet Lakshana who reached out for the garland from a tray in a sakhi's hand.

Brihatsena came over to bless his daughter and her husband-to-be. He held Krishna's head between his hands and planted a kiss on the crown of his head. 'I am the happiest man in the world today. I could not have chosen a better husband for Lakshana than you, Krishna Vaasudeva. I had heard so much about you, and had been following your activities for some time now. I admire your courage and commitment to rectitude in public life,' he said.

The wedding was fixed for a week later. Krishna and his cousins moved into the guest house within the palace premises as the king's personal guests, sending back a part of their retinue to convey news of the development to their family and friends in Indraprastha.

'Oh, it's so nice here! I am so happy to have you all as my vahnis. And there is so much to share,' Bhadra said, adjusting a cushion under her head as she lay comfortably on a settee in Rukmini's lounge.

'True! It is horrible to have brothers!' Mitravinda, who was stretched out on a carpet, said, making a face at the memory of her two brothers back in Ujjaini.

'I agree,' Rukmini, who had just entered the room, said, settling down next to Mitra. 'Brothers are very dominating and want to run their sisters' lives.'

'That is too sweeping a statement, Vahni,' objected Kalindi. 'You only need to look at Subhadra's brothers to understand what I mean.

'And, you know, I have not known either a sister or brother in my life. In fact, it was only on rare occasions that I heard conversations. I only knew to pray and wait for Krishna to come and claim me. And I spoke to Brother Arjuna before I met Krishna. Coming into contact with the Pandava brothers and Ma Kunti was like meeting my long-lost family,' she said.

'I know what you mean, Kalindi,' Jambavati said. 'I come from a similar background like yours. You lived in the waters of Yamuna and I lived in a dark cave with my father. I was also told to pray for Shree Hari to come and take me away. Meeting Rukmini Vahni was a revelation to me. Without saying one word she taught me to love and give selflessly.'

Rukmini laughed with a tinge of self-consciousness. 'You are so sweet and unspoilt, Jamba, that it is impossible not to love you.'

'Where is Satyabhama Vahni? Why does she not come and sit with us?' Bhadra asked in her typical chirpy childlike voice.

Rukmini placed a restraining hand on Bhadra's knee. 'She lost her father under tragic circumstances, Bhadra. He has been killed by some people. That is among the various things that our husband is trying to resolve and that is the reason Satya does not feel very sociable these days.'

'How terrible!' said Bhadra, and everybody agreed with her. Conversation veered to other topics and they resolved to spend more time with Satyabhama and help her overcome her grief.

It had been almost a month since Krishna returned to Dwaraka with five new wives in tow. Devaki and Vasudeva also returned. Subhadra, who had eloped with Arjuna, had come back to her parental home along with her young son, Abhimanyu. It was an emotional moment for everyone. Kunti Devi found the parting particularly painful. Her brother and sister-in-law Vasudeva and Devaki, in whose company she could freely unburden her travails, were leaving. Krishna, who had stood by them in all their troubles, was leaving. Her precious grandson Abhimanyu would be parted from her, and the five wives of Krishna, whom she had come to love like her own daughters, would be gone.

Krishna was compassion personified as he consoled his aatya. He told her that relationships blossomed only when there were periods of separation. She would, in any case, have her hands full with caring for the Pandava *Pattamahishi* or principal queen Draupadi. It was important to provide the mother-to-be with adequate rest and keep her healthy and happy so that she gave birth to a happy and healthy child. He promised to take very good care of Abhimanyu. He exhorted the Pandavas to concentrate on good governance and promoting dharma.

The five girls who entered Krishna's life within the span of one year—Kalindi, Mitravinda, Nagnajiti, Bhadra and Lakshana—nursed their own apprehensions regarding the shift to Dwaraka. They had got used to Indraprastha. With the motherly affection showered on them by Kunti and Devaki, all of them had felt at home. The five Pandavas, though very different from one another, were the same when it came to their treatment of Krishna's wives. All of them received the affection that is due to a sister, and were treated like family members.

In Dwaraka, it could not be the same. For waiting there were three former wives of their husband. Would they resent the new wives? Would they be made to feel unwanted and unwelcome? What would Krishna's attitude be towards them in Dwaraka? Did he love Rukmini best? Or was Satyabhama his favourite? Having spent more than one year away from three of them, would he feel obliged to give them more attention? Would that translate into their own neglect?

Their apprehensions strengthened through the journey, which took almost a week. They hardly saw Krishna. He spent all his time running between his parents and Subhadra. The short intervals he had away from both were taken up with checking on arrangements for their basic requirements of food and resting places along the way. Krishna hardly slept or rested during this week and would make an occasional enquiry about their comfort. He probably gave slightly more attention to Lakshana, the youngest and newest of his wives.

Nagnajiti tried to dispel their despondency. Krishna was preoccupied with ensuring a comfortable journey for them all. 'Swasura and Swasruva are elderly and are likely to be more tired than any of us. Nanandi Subhadra is with an infant, and therefore requires greater help on the journey,' she pointed out. While the others could not deny the innate truth of this argument, they were however, not fully convinced.

All their complaints against Krishna dissolved into thin air on the day they reached Dwaraka. Rukmini had ensured a perfect welcome for them all. She personally escorted her co-wives to their individual quarters and showed them around and explained the way their personal belongings, which had been delivered much earlier, had been arranged. She promised to make alterations and additions as desired by them. Jambavati followed her like a shadow and rushed around fetching and conveying messages.

While these arrangements gave them little to complain about, what impressed Krishna's new wives was the open affection and acceptance that Rukmini and Jambavati showed towards them. There was not even a trace of jealousy or resentment about having to share their husband's time and affection with so many others.

Satyabhama alone was aloof. She was at the entrance to welcome them, but there was no welcoming smile on her face. Devaki and Vasudeva took her away almost immediately. This seemed perplexing at the time, but now, with the reason disclosed to them by Rukmini, they could appreciate Satya's situation. It must be terrible to have your father murdered!

And then, there was Krishna! Relaxed and loving as ever! He had time for each of them, the demands on his time from so many Mukhyas and commoners of the Janapada, notwithstanding. He enjoyed walking on the seashore, particularly on moonlit nights when the tide was high and the waters shimmered with moonlight reflecting off its waves.

This was raas of a different kind, Rukmini explained to her co-wives during one of their frequent chat sessions in her room.

Rukmini had a very busy schedule, since she was the one who kept the establishment running. Till now it was only Jambavati who had assisted Rukmini in some measure. As the days passed, Mitravinda, Bhadra, Nagnajiti and Lakshana started sharing her responsibilities. Initially, Kalindi was apprehensive and hesitant about offering help. She believed that she lacked the necessary skills to perform the tasks involved in running a large household, but soon, with encouragement from Rukmini, she picked up and contributed her might.

'What is raas?' asked Kalindi. Rukmini explained that Krishna, when he was young and living in Vrindavan, used to indulge in raasleela with the gopikas. Krishna played music on his murali and all gopikas, irrespective of their age, would dance around him, mesmerized by his music. The raas was performed especially on full moon nights on the banks of Yamuna. It was magical as each gopika felt that Krishna was dancing with her alone.'

'Does he perform raas now also?' Kalindi was curious.

'No. He gave it up when he moved out of Vrindavan and came to Mathura. His responsibilities increased. He also missed Radha, who was his best friend and identified with him completely.

'But now, when we walk along the sea with him, there is a similar magic. Each of us gets the feeling that he is constantly walking by me. That is Krishna's magic,' she laughed.

Satyabhama's world came crashing down. She had been let down by her own husband, Krishna. She could have taken an insult, if it had happened in the privacy of her quarters, just between themselves. But the insult was public! Her humiliation complete!

She had to do something about it. Satya sat up straight. She motioned to one of her servants to speak. She had to hear it all over again to understand its implications. Only then would she be able to plan her strategy to counter the damage.

'Devi, I was right there when Narada *Maharshi* came. Prabhu and Rukmini Devi together washed his feet...'

'Never mind all that. Come to the point. Give me the details about the Parijata flower,' Satya cut her short.

'Devi, I will tell you exactly what happened.' Another maid came forward to speak. 'Narada Maharshi took out a flower he had tucked between the strings of his veena and gave it to Krishna Vaasudeva Prabhu. And he said, "Give it to your best queen."'

'No, no, that is not what the sage said. His exact words were "Give it to your best queen and the one whom you love best." That is what he said, I swear on my life,' said another maid.

'Devi, you cannot appreciate the real import of the Parijata flower, if you do not know exactly what happened. I had no work there, but had gone there just to be able to see what was happening there. First, Narada said that he was coming from Indra Loka. He had picked up this Parijata flower that had fallen off the tree...'

'No! He said that he had plucked it from the tree. This is the heavenly flower Parijata; it does not fall off the tree ever...'

'You are all brainless girls; you get into a tizzy to come back and report to Satyabhama Devi, and in the process forget vital details,' a senior maid admonished them.

Satyabhama felt like hurling the first thing within her reach at them all. Here she was consumed by worry and sorrow at Krishna slighting her in front of Rukmini, and all that these servants could do was to squabble about pointless details. But she controlled her impulse. Informers always had the tendency to exaggerate and impute importance to themselves. She had to be patient and listen to everything that each of them said and then sift the information. 'Vasanta, you give your account first. None of the others will interrupt her. I will hear each one of you, because I know that there is a special point noticed by each of you. I know that it is not possible for any single person to see and remember everything.'

Vasanta, the senior maid threw a triumphant look at the other maids, and launched into her narration with a flourish, 'Sage Narada gave the Parijata flower to His Highness Krishna and said... mark my words, Devi, for these were his exact words: "Give this flower to the best among your queens and one you love best." Yes, I swear on my life, these were his very words. They hit me like arrows in the heart when your husband tucked the flower into that Rukmini's hair,' Vasanta's last words were drowned in her sobs. She wept as if she had been insulted personally.

'Yes Devi, that is how it happened. The worst part was the way Rukmini's maids celebrated. They behaved as if they themselves had come down from heaven. They looked at us as if we were scum. In fact, one of them had the temerity to announce loudly that this was proof that her Devi is best loved by her husband,' another one said and lent her sobs to the first one.

'I could not bear to stand there for a minute when I saw Prabhu put a hand on Rukmini Devi's shoulder and say, "You alone are fit to have this divine flower."'

'And then, the look of absolute adoration in our Prabhu's eyes when he adorned Rukmini's hair with that flower! I could not believe my eyes! This cannot be our Prabhu! He who will do anything to bring a smile to our Devi's face! I even pinched myself to see that I was witnessing reality and not dreaming.'

Satya could not take it anymore. She dismissed them from her presence, with instructions to her senior maid to pay them all for the information they had brought and collapsed, her mind numb. What should she do?

What had she not done to ensure that Krishna loved her the best! What effort had she spared to make people acknowledge that Krishna was committed to Satyabhama! What did she lack that Krishna never quite came into her grip?

This Rukmini! What does she have? She is but a dowdy woman who toils more like a servant than behave like a queen. Takes no care of her looks! And I dress well, I take care of how I look; in fact I take particular care to make myself more alluring to my husband. Rukmini had eloped to marry Krishna. So she brought no riches into Krishna's household. She came in the clothes she stood in and Krishna had to provide everything to her. Rukmini's family was opposed to Krishna and therefore had not even attempted a rapprochement.

And she, Satyabhama, in contrast, had brought riches that far outdid the riches brought as trousseau by the four other princesses that Krishna had married. Mitravinda, Bhadra Devi, Nagnajiti and Lakshana were all from royal backgrounds and their families did try to send them off ceremoniously with enough assets. And she, though not a princess, had brought in more wealth than all these four put together. Her father had left her a fortune, and also the Syamantaka mani that could produce huge quantities of gold on a daily basis.

In addition, she had always helped Krishna with his various missions; she had contributed in cash and kind to ensure that his missions never suffered for want of resources. She had also learned to manage chariots, be a good archer and be able to fight battles.

Despite all this, today, when Krishna was called upon to show who he loved best, he selected Rukmini! How does she qualify for that position? And how could Krishna ignore her?

Krishna! Yes, it is Krishna that is to be blamed! He did not understand how much she strived to be his favourite. Where was the need for him to marry all those girls in such a tearing hurry? If only he had not gone to Indraprastha! If only he had not stayed on there for so long! Yes, that was the problem. He had been away from her for too long. She, who till then was the 'new bride', had been forgotten in the allure of his later wives.

Why, oh why did Krishna have to marry so many women? Once he got her as his wife, did he lack anything? Was there anything more he could desire in a wife?

Even when he returned with all his new wives, she had not been idle. She had worked ceaselessly to regain her position on the top of the list. She had handpicked reliable maids to act as her informers; planted them in the private quarters of Krishna's other wives. She also ensured that her own maids regularly visited their quarters, made friends with the maids there and picked up every possible bit of information to report back to her.

All her efforts had been in vain.

But she would not accept defeat. She would ensure that Krishna learned his lesson for insulting her, Satyabhama resolved, and set to work.

Krishna arrived at Satyabhama's palace later that evening. He, of course, could guess that she would have been told about him giving the Parijata flower to Rukmini. Satya would be upset, he knew, given the intense sense of competition she harboured in her bosom. He would have to coax and cajole her back into a happy frame of mind.

Krishna found Satya's palace in complete darkness. The doors were open, but there was none to receive him or welcome him. He made his way through the corridors, calling out her name and checking room after room, but Satyabhama was nowhere. Krishna smiled as he gently pushed the door of an ante-room in Satya's bed chamber.

'Bhama!' he called softly. There was no reply, but Krishna sensed her presence. He made his way carefully to the lone bed in one corner of the room, picking up the pieces of Bhama's jewellery he stumbled against.

'You are angry with me, I know. But why do you punish your jewellery?' Krishna opened the window to let some light in, placed the pieces he had picked up on a table and sat by Bhama on the bed.

Bhama pushed him off. 'Please do not feel obliged to come and spend time with ordinary people like me. Go and be with those who are the "best" and "most" beloved to you.'

'What are you talking about, Bhama? I am with my most beloved wife.'

'You are a liar; a thief. You were always that. Telling lies is a part of your character. You hand over a divine flower to someone when told to give it to a befitting person and then come here and speak untruths just to make a fool of me.'

'That is unfair, Bhama! Why will I lie to you? When I say you are my precious love, I mean it.'

'I do not trust you. I am not a gullible gopika to be taken in by your sweet talk.'

'That is the real problem, Bhama. Lack of trust! I never let down anyone who trusts me. You trust the maids who carry tales to you, but not my word. I knew then itself that you would be fed a twisted version of what happened at Rukmini's palace. Be fair and tell me. If a venerated sage like Narada gives me a flower and says give it to a wife you love, can I ignore Rukmini who is there by my side? Would it not be a grave insult to her?'

'You are twisting facts. Narada asked you to give it to your most beloved wife, and you gave it to her.'

'Why do you give so much weight to Narada's words? He is a brahmachari, who knows nothing about love and giving gifts to loved ones. I gave the flower to Rukmini because she deserves it. If you want a similar gift, just say so. I will bring the Parijata tree from heaven and plant it here in your courtyard.'

'Will you really do that? Bring the Parijata tree for me?'

'Yes.'

'When?'

'Later. Please do not tie me down to a timeframe. But trust me; I keep my word.'

'What! What are you blabbering? Are you out of your mind?' Satyabhama shouted at her maid who brought her the information.

'No, Devi! I heard it with my own two ears. I was there,' she said.

Satyabhama could still not believe it. 'Vasanta, sit down. Close your eyes and breathe deep. Think! Now tell me exactly what Uddhava said. Remember, I will skin you alive if I find that you are telling tales.'

'Devi! I swear on my life that I am not speaking one word that is not true. I was getting Prabhu's meeting room cleaned when he came in. It was very early and normally he does not come there at that time. I was hurrying the girls to finish work fast, but Prabhu told us all to leave immediately. I lingered behind the curtains, seeing that he had his brother, Uddhava Deva, with him. And it was my luck that I was near to where they sat down, for they spoke very softly. Even so I had to prick my ears and listen carefully to hear anything…'

'Enough! Go and get back to work. But let me not hear that you opened your mouth again about this,' Satyabhama dismissed the maid.

How could it be that the Pandavas were back in the jungles? She must get to the bottom of this. Satyabhama stepped out, still unsure how she could confirm this information, when she walked into Mitravinda and Bhadra strolling in the garden. She told them the news and together they called Nagnajiti and Lakshana. It was a serious development and only Krishna could give them the correct picture of how it all had happened. Mitravinda rushed off to call Rukmini, Jambavati and Kalindi to join them in Krishna's meeting room.

Krishna was not surprised when his eight wives walked into the room used for receiving visitors. He nodded in response to their unasked question: 'Yes, the Pandavas have been exiled for 12 years.'

'What happened?' The question came from Kalindi, who had developed deep bonds of affection with Kunti Devi and her family during her year-long stay at Indraprastha.

'The Pandavas went to Hastinapura on invitation from Duryodhana for a game of dice. Yudhishtira played on behalf of the Pandavas and lost everything. Even Draupadi was lost in this wager.'

'What kind of a game was this? I have seen *Jeshtha Bhrata* play dice. He is extremely good at it. It is not possible for him to lose like this, not if the game was fair,' Nagnajiti said thoughtfully.

'You are right. It was not a fair game. Duryodhana's Mamaka, Shakuni has magical dice, dice that he can control with his mind.'

'How could they wager their wife?' was Mitravinda's shocked question.

'That was not all. When Yudhishtira lost the round, Duryodhana ordered that Draupadi be brought into the public court. His brothers dragged her by her hair and tried to disrobe her,' Krishna's voice was thoughtful, but without emotion.

Krishna's wives received this information in stunned silence. 'How...how could that happen... What were the elders doing... Did no one stop it?' Rukmini clearly felt Draupadi's pain.

'Unfortunately, no one—neither Bhishma Pitamaha, Drona Acharya, Vidura or Dhritarashtra—protested. But while the humiliation cannot be denied, Draupadi's honour was saved. Also, Queen Gandhari intervened and condemned the act squarely. Humiliation to a daughter-in-law was humiliation to the entire family, she said, and forced her husband to recall the Pandava brothers and restore to them their freedom and everything else they had lost.'

'But you said the Pandavas have been exiled for 12 years,' Jambavati seemed confused.

'Yes. King Dhritarashtra invited them for another game of dice and this time the wager was that the losing party will spend 12 years in *aranyavas* (living in the forest) and one year in *agyatvas*, incognito. Discovery during the agyatvas will entail a repetition of the 12-year exile and twelve months of agyatvas. Yudhishtira lost this round too and...'

'Please, Nath! It is all very confusing. Tell us exactly what happened. We learnt that Uddhava brought information about these developments to you. How did he get all this information?' Rukmini said and looked around, seeking support from her co-wives. They all nodded.

'I realized this when Panchali called out to me for protection. I sent Uddhava to find out what was happening between the Kuru cousins. By the time he reached, the second game of dice had been played and the Pandavas were leaving for aranyavas...

'Uddhava brought the five Upa-Pandavas to Dwaraka with him. They will stay here with Subhadra and Abhimanyu and be educated and trained in martial arts along with their step-brother Abhimanyu. Aatya Kunti Devi has been persuaded to remain in Hastinapura with Queen Mother Satyavati Devi.'

Mitravinda interrupted him, 'Why did Draupadi have to suffer this humiliation...this humiliation of being disrobed in full assembly in the presence of all the elders? And what happened to the Pandava-Bhratvaja Krishna; Krishna who brought them back to life and protected them... What happened to that Krishna when they were being cheated out of their kingdom and everything else that was theirs?'

Mitravinda was breathing heavily in agitation and looked accusingly at her husband. Krishna could see that she spoke for all her co-wives.

'Yudhishtira has to take responsibility for the consequences of his actions. Nobody can negate them or neutralize them,' Krishna said.

'No! No *Swami*, no! You cannot wash your hands off like this. You admit it was an unfair game; you admit that the Pandavas were cheated; you know that *Jeshtha Bhrata* acts strictly in accordance with dharma. You say that spreading dharma is your life's mission. If that is true, then how can you shirk responsibility for this undharmic action?' Mitravinda was beside herself and hardly paid heed to what she was saying. It was her anguished heart speaking. Bhadra and Jambavati tried to restrain her.

Krishna had a distant look in his eyes as he answered the question. 'Yes, Yudhishtira is a stickler for dharma. It was his interpretation of dharma which was off-mark this time. According to Yudhishtira, it is against raja-dharma to refuse a friend's invitation for a friendly game of dice. He is right. But here, the hosts were not "friends"; nor was the game "friendly". Duryodhana's mother Gandhari saved the situation and had the game nullified and had everything lost by Pandavas restored to them. But then, Yudhishtira received a second invitation. Having had one bad experience, he could have, in fact, should have rejected the invitation and not participated in the same game once again. But since the invitation this time was from his Pitruvya Dhritarashtra, Yudhishtira thought it would be impolite to refuse. That was his interpretation of his dharma.'

'Does that mean that Yudhishtira alone is to be blamed for what happened?' the soft-spoken Lakshana asked, trying to analyze the entire episode.

'Attempting to fix responsibility for adharma in this incident would be like picking holes in a fishing net. The intention of the invitation was against dharma; the use of possessed dice for the game was against dharma; the silent support of the king to this event was against dharma. The silence of the likes of Bhishma, Drona and Vidura was against dharma.'

'There must be a reason for their silence,' Lakshana persisted.

'Yes. In the court where King Dhritarashtra is presiding, the position of all these three elders is that of mere courtiers; servants to the king, and going against the king's wish is against their *sevaka-*dharma.' Krishna looked directly at Lakshana. 'Dharma does not have a definite definition or meaning. It can be interpreted differently by different persons and differently by the same person under a different set of circumstances. Uddhava tells me that there is a strong public perception even now that the conduct of Bhishma was against dharma; that Yudhishtira himself misinterpreted dharma in agreeing to the game of dice.'

Satyabhama spoke for the first time that morning. 'This discussion about dharma–adharma of individual actions can only interest academicians. For me, this is what it means: The Pandavas have stood by dharma at all times. In return, they have had to live in the wilds and endure hardships. It is the same story this time also. In contrast, the Kauravas, who never cared for dharma, and flouted it blatantly several times, are living in the lap of luxury; they wield power as kings. Why?'

'You can achieve nothing if this is how you see problems. Do not look at dharma through individuals or incidents. Persons come and go; dharma is permanent. There is a general tendency to interpret dharma on the basis of one incident or one person and his or her problems.

'Circumstances may develop so as to give the impression that dharma is lost and that adherence to dharma only leads to creating more problems and hardship. If this happens, understand that dharma has become dormant for some reason; that dharma will emerge sooner or later.

'The main danger to dharma arises from kings and those who hold positions of power. These people have large egos; their priorities are determined by their selfish interests. They harbour immense jealousy and hatred and are fearful of losing their position.'

'Is it not the duty of kings to uphold and nurture dharma? If they flout it, how will dharma take root and spread?' Jambavati asked.

'Remember that time, people or circumstances cannot destroy dharma. Dharma can be nurtured only through education and awareness.'

Satyabhama paced up and down her bedchamber. She could have kicked herself for not thinking something like this. She hated defeat. She could never accept defeat. Now she felt defeated. Why did she not think of something like this, she beat her brow with the palm of her hand. If not thinking of it herself was bad, it was rendered worse by the fact that Rukmini had thought of it and acted on it.

Rukmini had invited the entire family over to her place for a feast—Devaki–Vasudeva, Revati–Balarama, Akrura–Sutanu, Uddhava and his two wives Kapila and Pingala, Rukmini's seven co-wives and other prominent persons of the city. She was celebrating her birthday, she said. It was quite some time that the Vaasudeva household had celebrated anything. Times had turned dreary following the banishment of the Pandavas to the woods. Krishna had made a couple of visits to see how they were doing and spent some time with them bolstering their confidence and tendering advice about what they should concentrate on. He foresaw war with the Kauravas at the end of their exile and urged the Pandavas to be ready for battle. He advised them to try and augment their arsenal by securing *divyaastras* or divine weapons from the Devas.

Satyabhama knew that the birthday was just an excuse for celebration. In all these years since she had come into the family,

Rukmini had hardly ever celebrated the day. Vasudeva and Devaki, Balarama and Revati had come to Dwaraka from Kushasthali, where Balarama had succeeded his Swasura Raivata as king.

She wondered how none of the others saw through the scheming Rukmini's little games—games she played often to portray herself as this angel in human form; the loving, caring mother-figure without whom the Krishna Vaasudeva household would collapse! They were all only too happy to comply with her orders.

She had always opposed the undue importance Rukmini got from everyone. Because of this, she was made to feel completely isolated among Krishna's wives. She could never understand what they saw in Rukmini! That too, when they could join forces with her! It was not as if she had not tried. She had targeted Bhadra, Mitravinda, Lakshana and Kalindi individually, as they seemed more amenable to suggestions, trying to expose Rukmini and make them turn away from her. They did not heed her words. On the contrary, they began avoiding her.

But that was understandable, of course! They felt inadequate in her presence. None of them had the kind of looks she had, or wealth. And Krishna! He doted on her. He went to great lengths to fulfill her every wish. Unfortunately, her co-wives did not know it. They were happy with what attention they got from him. It would be very satisfying if they all acknowledged her as their husband's favourite wife. That could happen only if Krishna demonstrated his love for her in public, or ignored the other wives. Then she would have them groveling in front of her, pleading with her to recommend them to Krishna.

In fact, this was one aspect on which her informer maids were to report on. It was frustrating not to have ever got even a single report of angry exchanges, fights, or tears and pleadings. In fact, reports from other palaces generated doubts about her own position vis-a-vis their husband. And everytime she had such doubts, she took immediate steps to secure reiteration of her husband's commitment to her. He provided it, but...

She remembered the incident with the Parijata flower some years ago. He had gifted it to Rukmini but cajoled her back to good humour with a promise that he would bring her the Parijata tree. She had let that promise recede into the background in recent years on account of Pandavas' exile.

But how was she to deal with Rukmini's birthday celebrations? There, Krishna would stand by her and she would have to remain in the background with the rest of the wives. Rukmini and Krishna would stand together as a couple, seek blessings from elders and give gifts to all others. It would be a humiliation that she could not take.

She sent for Vasanta. Talking to this old trusted maid could throw up some ideas. It worked. Vasanta came up with a brilliant idea. 'Devi, what you need is something that will shift the venue of the celebration from Rukmini Devi's palace to your palace here. But the reason for the celebration should be strong enough to warrant this change,' she said and pondered for a while. 'Of course, how could I forget! It is a very important day in your life, Devi—today is the day you were married. It is your wedding anniversary. You must celebrate it.'

Satyabhama's spirits soared. What a fantastic idea! She knew she could depend upon Vasanta. But...'Vasanta, can you make all arrangements in such a short time?' She had no doubt about her persuasive abilities on Krishna. How could anyone say that a wedding anniversary is less important than a birthday!

'Of course, Devi! You know how devoted I am to you. I can lay down my life for you. Now I must rush and put everyone to work to have a great event that will be everyone's envy,' Vasanta went away.

Satyabhama called her back. 'I have a better idea. We will not invite any outsider. It will be a special celebration for my beloved husband. Make arrangements for an intimate, alluring feast just for Krishna,' she said and went looking for her husband. Krishna was with Uddhava and engaged in deep discussion. Satyabhama waited to catch his eye. 'Nath! You must come to my palace this evening. Today is our wedding day. I entered your household on this day so many years ago. I have arranged a small celebration for the two of us. You can, of course invite any of your friends, if you so wish,' she said.

'But there is a feast at Rukmini's palace today.'

'I don't care. You cannot displease me today. You must come to me.'

'Bhama, Rukmini invited me first, and I told her I would be there.'

'Oh, but I did not know about that,' Satyabhama said, feigning surprise. 'I am sure you will find a way out of it.'

'No, Bhama. That would be unfair to her. She must have made all arrangements. She said my parents and several other family members would be there. It will be awkward if I am not there with her to receive them.'

Satyabhama fluttered her eyelids seductively. 'It is not a question of who invited you first, my dear husband, but who is more important to you,' she smiled.

'My parents will take offence if I am not with them.' Krishna tried to shift focus from Rukmini to his parents.

'I too will take offence if you are not with me. It is a different matter if you do not want to be with me.' Satyabhama's voice hardened. Her ego was being challenged; she was close to tears.

Krishna felt sorry for her. 'Bhama, where is the question of me not being with you. You know how much I love you. Let me first go to Rukmini's feast. Then I will come to you straight from there,' he said and walked off without another backward glance.

30

'Narayana, Narayana!'

The signature chant announcing the arrival of Sage Narada was lost on Satyabhama. A nudge from Vasanta and a slightly sharper 'Narayana, Narayana' brought her to the present. She went through the motions of *arghya-padya*, giving water for washing hands and feet of the sage but her heart was not in it. She informed Narada that Krishna was not home and waited for him to leave. But the sage settled comfortably in Bhama's porch.

Satyabhama had been sitting there ever since Krishna walked out on her, rejecting her invitation to a feast with her to celebrate her wedding day. Instead he went to Rukmini's birthday feast. It was a clear statement of Krishna's preferences among his wives. He loved Rukmini best and she, Satyabhama, stood nowhere. She had collapsed into a chair right there on the porch and there she remained in a stupefied state ever since.

Narada sat silently, strumming on his veena softly. When he spoke after some time, his voice was as soft as the notes of his veena. 'I did not see you in Rukmini Devi's palace. So I came over here. Oh! What a feast! And all arrangements so thorough! Krishna was the perfect host; he acted on the slightest cue from Rukmini Devi and ensured that the guests were well looked after. What a perfect couple!'

Satyabhama could take it no more. 'Enough Maharshi, enough!

I do not want to hear anything about that feast,' she spoke through clenched teeth, and put both hands on her ears, trying to shut out the words.

'Why Satya Devi, why?'Narada sounded surprised. 'Are you not well? Are you upset over something?'

Satyabhama was moved to tears with this solicitous question. Narada was the first person to come and check on her, noticing her absence at Rukmini's feast. None of her co-wives had thought to come to her. She poured her heart out. '*Muneeshwara*! My life is a waste. What is the point in living if you are not loved by your husband? Oh, what have I not done to make him love me as much as I love him! But I suppose these troubles are normal for women who have to compete with several co-wives.'

'I cannot believe that it is Satyabhama Devi saying these words! The whole world knows Krishna as Satyabhama's obedient husband. "Satya-Pati", he is called! Your slightest wish, it is said, is his command. So I wonder... Am I dreaming?'

'No, *Maharshi*, you are not dreaming. The truth is that Krishna does not value me.'

'That just cannot be true. You are the most beautiful, most talented and richest among Krishna's wives...'

'See! You acknowledge the truth. But not Krishna Vaasudeva. How can he? He is after all a mere cowherd from Vrindavan. How can he understand a woman's love?'

'That cannot be true! Krishna is considered the most desirable man in the world. There is not one woman who has not lost her heart to him. Not one woman who has not dreamt of having him as her husband. How can he not know, not understand your love?'

Satyabhama looked at the sage with suspicious eyes. 'If that is true, then why does he humiliate me repeatedly in front of all my co-wives? Remember the time you brought that Parijata flower?

You told him specifically to give it to the best among his wives, and he gave it…no, personally adorned Rukmini's hair with it. I often wonder if they have done something to set him against me; to make him forget me or neglect me.'

Satya perked up and added, 'Maharshi, the more I think about it, the more I am convinced that something like this has happened. Otherwise, I cannot imagine that Krishna, who is always telling me how much he loves me, how he likes to spend all his time with me, how he cannot imagine acting against my wishes, do exactly that. What do you think?' She waited expectantly.

'I am not really qualified to talk on matters of this kind. I am a brahmachari. If you think that this is the case, you can take steps to counter its effects. After all, you are very capable. You have the means. So, do what you think fit.'

Satyabhama's spirits rose. 'Do you think I can…that I can do something? But I don't know how it can be done. Please help me, Maharshi! Tell me of some effective ritual that will secure my husband's total commitment to me. Please help me.' Satya leaned forward in anticipation.

'Of course I will help you, Satyabhama Devi. I understand and appreciate your concerns and desires. I know of a vrata, which is intended to bind the husband completely to the wife. It is called the *"Punyaka Vrata"*. It makes the husband submit himself completely into his wife's control.'

'Maharshi! This is exactly what I want. I will perform this vrata immediately. I will do it irrespective of any difficulty, expenditure, or anything else. I also request you to conduct it for me.'

'Devi, this vrata is seemingly simple to perform. But there is always a tough part at the end, the final step that completes the vrata and grants you its fruit.'

'I do not mind any difficulty. I will go through any trouble to get my husband to surrender completely to me. Just tell me what I have to do,' Satyabhama said enthusiastically.

'Be warned, Devi. The concluding part, if not complied with in letter and spirit, can have dangerous repercussions.'

'Maharshi, please rest assured. I am prepared to go through any difficulty. Please tell me what I have to do.'

'It involves obeisance to the primordial couple Lakshmi and Narayana on the eleventh day of a waxing moon cycle of any month. At the end of the ritual, you have to make a *"maha-daan"*, a huge donation, to a worthy Brahmin.'

'That does not sound too difficult, Maharshi. With you conducting the rituals for me, I do not have to look anywhere else for a worthy Brahmin for this donation. Just tell me what I must give. With the limitless wealth at my disposal, I am sure I can give you anything you desire.'

'You have to give away your husband; *pati-daan*.'

Satyabhama was stunned. 'Pati-daan? How can you even suggest it Maharshi, when the purpose of the vrata is to gain control over the husband?'

The sage laughed at her expression. 'How gullible can you be, Devi! The donation is only a formality. The moment it is done, you can reclaim your husband by giving away his weight in gold. Once this procedure is completed, the husband is under total control of the wife.'

'Then it is fine. I have enough gold,' Satyabhama said.

'Of course, you are a very rich person. However, the rules of the vrata do provide that, in the absence of enough gold to weigh the husband with, anything else may be used to make up for the shortfall.'

'We do not have to consider that situation at all. Thanks to my Syamantaka gem, I have immense reserves of gold.'

'Then there is no problem. We can proceed with the vrata.

But let me tell you one last condition for the vrata. I would not want to be faulted for not giving the full information about the conditionalities of this particular vrata. In the event of the wife failing to weigh him, he can be claimed by somebody else, provided he or she gives something equal to his weight in exchange. Should this happen, then he will become obedient to that person and not to the one who performed the vrata.'

'I have no need for this condition. I have more than enough gold.'

'Please think, Devi. Are you sure you have enough gold to weigh Krishna? I do not want to be blamed, if you fail to have enough gold.'

Satyabhama laughed. 'I cannot believe that you are getting so nervous about this vrata. Maharshi, I am Satrajit's daughter and still have a lot of gold produced by the Syamantaka. I know how much my husband weighs and how much gold I have. I have no worries about my ability to claim him in exchange for gold. I suggest that you also stop worrying.'

'There is just one other condition, Satrajiti. Your husband must be agreeable to be gifted away.'

'No problem, Maharshi. I will tell him.'

'Do you think you should inform your co-wives of this? After all, he is as much husband to them as he is to you.'

'No, Maharshi. There is no need for any of them to know about this vrata. They are bound to oppose it. And anyway, they will not miss him at all, because the process of gifting him and reclaiming him will be over in a few minutes. So why invite trouble from them?'

Narada left with a promise he would return early next morning to conduct the *punyaka vrata*.

✤

'Shree Krishna; Govinda; Hari; Murari; Narayana; Vaasudeva; Madhusudana, Madhava…' Narada was chanting in ecstasy, strumming on his veena as accompaniment. Something unique had happened. In this unprecedented event, he, the *triloka-sanchari* Narada, had become the master of the master of the universe, even if it was only for a short while.

Satyabhama was busy adjusting cushions on one side of the weighing scales set up for the exchange. She did not want to hurt her husband while the weighing process was being conducted.

'Satyabhama Devi, please hurry up. It is not desirable that the "*Sutradhar*" of life is in bondage. Release him as per the terms agreed upon by us,' he said and continued with his chant, 'Shree Krishna; Govinda; Hari; Murari; Narayana; Vaasudeva; Madhusudana; Madhava…' By now, the veena acquired a life of its own and its very notes seemed to sound like these various names of the Lord.

Satyabhama's eyes widened in surprise. The gold bars she had kept ready to weigh her husband with, had been placed on the other side of the scales, but the needle failed to move. She ordered her maids to bring more gold bars from her personal treasury. More gold bars were loaded, but the needle still did not move. Krishna's side stayed firmly on the ground.

Satyabhama could not believe it. Was her husband really so heavy? More than a dozen gold bars, each so heavy that it needed at least four persons to be lifted, had been placed on the weighing scale. No change. The side with Krishna did not rise at all.

'Shree Krishna, Govinda; Hari; Murari; Narayana; Vaasudeva; Madhusudana; Madhava…'

Narada's chant now was full of wonder. He stopped strumming the veena. He stood there, hands folded in reverence.

Satya had another room unlocked and gold bars from there transported to where the vrata was being conducted. The dozen men who had brought the gold bars collapsed in fatigue.

'Satyabhama Devi, please hurry! You need to supply a lot more gold. See, the needle has not moved at all till now!' Narada was now getting impatient.

All the gold in Satyabhama's custody had been brought and loaded into the scales. Satyabhama's concern was turning into panic. What was she to do? In an act of utter futility, she removed all the jewellery she was wearing and added them to the mounds already in the scales.

'Satya Devi, I had told you to be doubly sure that you had enough gold to weigh Krishna. You said you had more than enough. Now you seem to have run out of gold. I cannot bear Shree Krishna as my slave even for a moment. However, since you obviously do not have enough gold to weigh Jagannatha, you can use something else, anything else. The only condition that cannot be changed is that you give something equal to his weight.

'Now I am worried that you may not be able to secure his release from my custody. What will I do with him? Krishna is used to luxurious living in palaces; and I have no roof over my head. I keep roaming the three worlds. I do not have the resources to maintain him even for a moment.'

Satyabhama was distraught. Almost everything in her palace had been brought and placed on the weighing scale. The needle did not move at all. Meanwhile, Narada was building more pressure. 'I will not like it if word gets out that I had the temerity to accept Shree Krishna in *daan*. You will also be in trouble for giving him away.

'Devi, this is the truth—I have no use for all this gold. I am a celibate monk and a wanderer. Whatever will I do with gold and other material things? I can just leave him and go away. But it would be wrong for you to retain what you have gifted away. You have created a major *dharma-sankat* (problem) for me,' Narada said.

Krishna was panicking too. He kept saying, 'Bhama! What is happening? You said this was a mere formality and that it would be done in the flick of a finger. Please don't abandon me. Do not make me follow this *sanyasi* around the three worlds. I cannot bear to be parted from you, Satya... Please Satya...'

Satyabhama looked from Narada to Krishna and back again at the sage as tears flowed from her eyes. 'What is happening, Maharshi? What is this *maya*? Is my husband really this heavy?'

'How am I to know, Devi? I had asked you repeatedly if you had enough gold or something else to weigh him. You were very confident that you did.'

'No, Maharshi, you tricked me into this! You, the all-knowing Narada, who can resolve any problem, have led me into a trap. You knew how it will all end...'

'Satya Devi! Please be careful with your words! I have not led you into this situation. It was your greed to be the sole focus of this *vishwa-bandhu* that is responsible for your situation. You treated him like a normal human being, a husband only to the eight of you. It did not ever occur to you that Shree Krishna is the bearer of this entire universe. And I thought that you, as his most-loving wife, the one who wanted to limit him to herself, was capable of achieving that objective. I was ready to accept anything—mud, hay, dry leaves—anything at all and release him. You were unable to do that.

'Anyway, let us not waste time talking. I cannot bear the burden of this sarvantaryami. Retaining him as my slave will tie me down to the earth. So I have to find someone who can give me an equivalent of his weight and take him as their slave. I want an end of this issue so that I can resume my roaming around the worlds.'

'Satya!' It was a piteous whimper from Krishna still seated on the scale. 'Please have me released. I am a peace-loving person, and now I am pushed into the custody of this *kalaha-bhoja*, who feasts on disputes. I know he is going to sell me off in the market place to anyone who can weigh me with anything. Satya, I would have been happy as your slave. I would not mind being slave to all eight of you; but to serve this sage or someone who buys me... Oh, Satya, even the thought is unbearable.'

Krishna brightened suddenly. 'Bhama, I have an idea—call in all your co-wives. It is possible that all of you together may reclaim me.'

Satyabhama nodded and looked at Vasanta standing by her. Vasanta took off like an arrow shot from a bow and soon returned with all the seven co-wives. Narada narrated the sequence of events and the condition for Krishna's release from bondage.

'Who gave you permission to gift him away? He is as much our husband as he is yours,' Bhadra Devi said, controlling her anger with difficulty.

'Now that she has failed to secure his release, can we take it that she has lost all claims to being his wife?' Lakshana analyzed the situation.

'Right you are. She has lost her claim,' Nagnajiti seconded Lakshana.

'That is beyond the point now. If all the gold produced by

the Syamantaka was unequal to get our husband back, which of us can hope to do that? Trying to weigh him with material riches is foolhardy,' Mitravinda said despairingly.

Kalindi spoke thoughtfully, 'Mitra is right. All our combined riches will not be able to weigh our Swami. No one can weigh Govinda. He is *sarvajagannatha*, Lord to the entire cosmos. It is a task that only *jagat-janani* can accomplish. We are lucky to have the *Jaganmayi* (one who fills the cosmos) among us—Rukmini vahni. But for her grace, none of us would have had the good fortune to become his wife in this *janma*.'

Nagnajiti added her voice to seek Rukmini's intervention to resolve the current problem. 'Vahni, we all call you and treat you as our elder sister, because that is our relationship with you in this world. However, we all know that you are *Jaganmata*, mother to the world. We owe our very existence to your grace. Nothing is beyond you. Please bestow your kindness on us and have our husband released from bondage.'

Jambavati showed her solidarity with the other wives by holding hands with them.

Satyabhama felt mortified at being treated as the guilty one by all the other wives. She acknowledged that she had erred. This outcome of the punyaka vrata was unexpected. But for this turn of events, she would have had Krishna dancing to her tunes. He would have completely forgotten his other wives and they would have been pleading with her to give them a few moments' access to him. These co-wives were spineless beings, always singing praises of Rukmini. What she did to deserve such unconditional servility from the remaining six, Satya could never fathom. And now, here they were, asserting ever so confidently that Rukmini would be able to weigh Krishna and reclaim him. What did Rukmini have to place on the scales? She came empty-handed and her father and brother never tried to provide her with anything in her marital home.

Satya felt torn between the frightening prospect of losing her husband, and this ridiculous plan that Rukmini, standing there with nothing in her hands, would rescue Krishna. On the face of it, it was a laughable proposition, with hardly any chance of success. But given her situation as the one who had not only failed in the task, but was squarely responsible for the situation, she could not counter them and their faith. She decided to wait and watch, even as one part of her mind was trying to come up with some course of action to salvage her reputation.

Rukmini stepped forth. She walked up to Krishna seated on the scales, folded her hands reventially and looked him straight in the eye. She then turned to Satyabhama and asked her to have everything that was loaded onto the scales, removed.

Satya was dumbstruck! Does Rukmini really think that she had enough gold reserves at her disposal that could be brought over to weigh Krishna? However, should this really happen, would Rukmini let her stay in their residential complex? Will she be shunted out? If that happened, where was she to go? How was she to cope with the humiliation?

While Satyabhama stood in stupefied inaction, her trusted aide Vasanta took over and had the scales cleared.

Rukmini walked over to the place where the Lakshmi–Narayana puja was conducted. She closed her eyes in a silent prayer for a moment and then picked up a *tulasi* leaf from among the offerings. She walked back to the scales, paused in front of her husband and said, 'If my love, trust and faith in this *sarva-lokadhesh* is complete and I be "Krishna–Pativrata", then this *tulasi* leaf, which I place on the scales with total devotion, should weigh as much as Prabhu.'

She then touched the *tulasi* leaf to her forehead and placed it on the empty scale. As everyone watched, the needle moved, Krishna's side of the scales rose and perfectly balanced the other side.

'Jai *Jaganmata*!' Narada folded his hands reverentially and bowed before Rukmini.

'Vaasudeva, this *sadhvi* (pious woman) imbued one small *tulasi* leaf with the power to weigh you. I will take this leaf and happily go on my way. From now on, on account of the rules of the just conducted punyaka vrata, you will be known as Rukmini-*pati*; Rukmini-lola,' Narada said and took leave, the chant of 'Narayana, Narayana!' on his lips.

It was a full moon night. The moon's shimmering light and the cool sea breeze whispering through thick foliage made the enchanting evening even more beautiful. Krishna and Rukmini were on a swing in her backyard. The swing rocked gently with the breeze. They had finished dinner and Rukmini was rolling her husband's *paan*. The couple was clearly at peace with each other and with their surroundings.

'Hope you are well and contented?'

Krishna raised himself into a sitting position, trying to identify the unexpected visitor. Rukmini also turned in the direction of the words.

'Ah, Jamba! How nice to see you!' Krishna exclaimed happily. 'I am always happy and contented,' he added mischievously with a hint of a smile in his cheerful voice.

Rukmini rose with a smile of welcome on her lips, and hurried to the doorway where Jambavati was standing. Surprised at seeing Kalindi and Nagnajiti standing behind Jambavati, she exclaimed, 'I must admit that I am surprised and honoured to receive all three of you.' She took another step forward with arms extended in welcome and with obvious surprise, greeted Mitravinda, Bhadra Devi and Lakshana with happy exclamations.

Krishna was immediately on his feet as a solicitous host, making inquiries to satisfy himself that there was no emergency. 'If you are all here for consultations with your vahni and find me an intrusion, then I can leave,' he offered.

'We are glad to have found both of you together. We have something to clarify with both,' Jambavati said, shaking off Krishna's hand as he tried to help her to a seat. Her manner of speaking and her stiff posture clearly showed that she was angry and upset. Nagnajiti and Lakshana closed ranks with her in a show of solidarity.

'Have I done something to annoy you? Please sit down and we can talk.' Rukmini's gentle appeal worked and the younger wives settled on small stools around the swing.

Krishna resumed his seat on the swing, but Rukmini stood by, looking around and waiting for her co-wives to articulate the purpose of their visit.

'Where is Satyabhama, Vahni?' Mitravinda's question was sharp. While she addressed Rukmini, Mitra made it clear that the question was for Krishna by looking straight into Krishna's eyes.

'Given the late hour of the day, I would assume that she would to be in her chambers,' Krishna's voice was casual.

'She is not; she is not there,' Bhadra almost shouted, panic in her voice.

Lakshana took it upon herself to bring clarity into the question. 'Nath! It is three days since Satyabhama Vahni performed the punyaka vrata. Vahni was definitely ill-advised about undertaking such a ritual, but her intention was above question. She wanted to receive the same amount of love and devotion as she bestowed on her husband. It is true that her failure to fulfill the conditions of the vrata endangered your very freedom.

'It is also true that Rukmini Vahni saved the situation for all of us. But does that mean that you spend all your time with your eldest Devi and ignore Satyabhama Vahni? Should she be shunned? Does she deserve this harsh treatment from either of you?' she said, looking from Krishna to Rukmini and back.

Krishna threw a triumphant look at Rukmini. She nodded happily and her smile embraced all her co-wives. 'Your accusations, though correct superficially, are unfounded. Satya has not been abandoned. She has only been left alone to sort out her frayed nerves and emotions and allow time for her hurt ego to heal.

'And all of you have made me a winner. Our dear husband had wagered with me that all of you will gloat on Satya's failure; that you will ridicule her for wanting to buy her husband's love with gold and berate her folly. I did not agree; I said that all of us love and respect Satya for what she stands for—her determination to secure what she sets her heart on, her commitment to measure up to any situation, and her self-confidence. I told him that you will all stand by her.

'That is why he did not let me meet any of you since that day. He also did not meet anyone as that could lead to some comments about the vrata.

'I also want to state another truth to you all today. Even without the punyaka vrata and despite its failure, Satrajiti is Krishna's favourite wife; has always been. So, actually, Satya did not need the punyaka vrata to get the love she so desperately wanted; she already has it.'

'How…what…how…' Bhadra was so dazed that she could not even form a sentence. The others just looked at Krishna and Rukmini in stunned silence.

Rukmini flashed an understanding smile. 'Satyabhama is *Swami's* earth element. She kept him grounded with various issues. If not for her, Swami will not be able to achieve the purpose of his avatar.'

Kalindi could not believe her ears. She had always credited Rukmini with being Krishna's soulmate. 'Then…then…what about you... You weighed him and so he should become enslaved to you,' she said in bewilderment.

'Swami is no one's slave. All of us—this entire universe—exists because of him. All of us, who have the good fortune of being his wives in this birth, also have similar roles in Swami's life. We all help him retain his human identity and also act as the foil to his divinity.'

'But... but... how is that possible, Vahni? You were the one who weighed Swami with just a *tulasi* leaf, when all of Satyabhama's riches failed.'

'Yes, tell us the secret of that fantastic feat,' Bhadra could not hide her curiosity.

'I will tell you how that happened,' Krishna intervened. 'Actually, it was no feat, no miracle.

'Narada is a great *bhakta*. His prayer is very powerful. He invoked Narayana, describing his thousand facets. His prayer awakened these thousand aspects that were dormant in me. I became Narayana himself and my weight magnified. Obviously, nothing could have equalled that weight.'

'Then how did Rukmini Vahni...' The question came from Satyabhama, who had walked in unnoticed by anyone. Lakshana reached out a hand and made her sit by her. Krishna continued.

'Rukmini realized what had happened. She looked into my eyes with all her devotion and love and imbibed the Narayana aspects into herself, leaving only Krishna in me. Then, she transferred all those aspects into the *tulasi* leaf. Rukmini is a *yogin*. Nothing is impossible for her. Nothing is beyond her.'

'Are you really God?' It was Satyabhama who whispered the question, her voice a combination of wonderment and serenity.

'Who is not God? All of us are but reflections of the same life force. We have different physical forms, but the sarvantaryami inside is the same, just like each drop of water is the same as every other drop of water in the pitcher, pond or river.'

'Do not talk in riddles. What is God; please explain clearly.' Mitravinda was impatient for a proper answer.

'God is nothing but the sum total of the essence of *prema, gyana* and *samardhya*—love, knowledge and skill—qualities present in all of us, the only difference being in degree. Humans, on account of their ego and the influence of material desires, fail to realize their potential for love, knowledge and skill. Those who rise above ego and understand who and what he or she is, is God.'

'What is ego?' It was Satyabhama again.

'The human birth is action-oriented. All humans commit good and bad actions. When death claims their bodies, the cumulative result of these deeds or *karma-phala* follows them. One has to take another birth to experience this result.'

'But then, they commit more actions and accumulate more karma-phala. Then they have to take yet another *janma* to experience that result. This makes for an unending cycle of birth and death. Is there a way out of it at all?' Jambavati was perplexed.

'There is a way out. It is the path of gyana, awareness. Being aware of what is good, what is bad, what is right and what is wrong, leads to diminished karma-phala. Also, keeping desire out of our actions will enable not only negation of karma-phala in the present, but also dissolves the karma-phala of the past.'

There was silence, each one lost in contemplation. Mitravinda spoke after a while.

'How about Krishna? You are present in different forms at the same time. You were separately with each gopika while performing raas, you were with me even as you were travelling with Arjuna, and so on. Are you responsible for all the actions in all those different forms?'

'Knowledge of who I am helps me keep my ego at a minimal level. That ego or personality is just enough to maintain my form. My actions are aimed at establishing dharma and are conducted in accordance with cosmic principles. Because there is a complete absence of desire for results (*nishkamya*) in these actions, I remain unaffected.'

'Do you mean to say that you perform all these actions with just a nominal personality?' Bhadra's eyes popped out in surprise.

'No, Bhadra! My nominal personality keeps me within this being called Krishna Vaasudeva. All my actions are performed by the sarvantaryami within me. Actually, all action in this world is a tussle between two opposing forces—conducive and adverse forces.'

'What about us, who have the great good fortune of being your wives and being with you at all times?' Kalindi asked.

'All beings are a part of me. If you see duality, it is because of your individual personality, your ego. If you rise above your ego, sink your personality, you will see that there is no difference between you and me. Everyone merges into me.'

'How do we rise above our egos?' Satyabhama asked.

'That can happen only through constant *sadhana* or practice.'

Rukmini voiced her concern, 'Swami, is there no respite, no release for the vast majority of people who are caught in action-oriented pursuits and given to strong desires?'

Krishna smiled benevolently.

'Being action-oriented or having desires is not wrong, my dear! In fact, it is desire that drives and sustains human life. There are very few people who realize their oneness with the sarvantaryami and strive to attain this merger with Him. We call them '*Divya Manavas*' or divine humans.

'A large number of humans are concerned solely with the protection of their own interests. They want to ensure that their families do not suffer, and strive to make life comfortable for them. Born as *manavas*, they live like *manavas*—*sadharana* or ordinary *manavas*.

'There is a third category of humans—this category is not satisfied with amassing riches for themselves and their children for this lifetime. Their desire overtakes their need and they derive pleasure in denying even basic needs to others. They actively work at snatching away other people's comfort and reduce them to slavery, making others dependent upon them for basic needs. These are *rakshasas*.'

'Do they have no help?' Rukmini despaired.

'Of course there is help for them; there is help for everyone. For, life itself is a tussle between sarvantaryami's propensity to create beings and his desire to merge them back into himself.

'So, he generates energy waves that facilitate and enable merger with the whole. These energy waves are present in the five elements—*bhumi* (earth); *jala* or *apa* (water); *agni* or *tejas* (fire); *marut* or *vayu* (wind) and *vyom* or *shunya*(sky). The energy waves are constantly moving in and out of our bodies.

'The process is so constant and continuous that an ordinary being cannot even feel them. However, those with a heightened consciousness can not only feel them but control what enters and what exits their bodies.

'The sarvantaryami himself facilitates the merger with himself. He comes as a person, a guru or an experience that sets humans on the path of this merger.'

ॐ

Relationship Terms

Bhagini: Sister

Bhagineya: Nephew—sister's son

Bhagineyi: Niece—sister's daughter

Bhavuka: Cousin—father's sister's son

Bhrata: Brother

Bhratvaja: Cousin—father's brother's son and mother's sister's son

Icchadhari: one who can change its form

Jamata: Son-in-law

Jameya: Nephew—brother's son

Jami: Daughter-in-law

Mahee and *Bapu*: Parents

Mamaka: Uncle—mother's brother

Matashree and *Pitashree*: Parents

Matrushya: Aunt—mother's sister

Matruvya: Uncle—mother's sister's husband

Nanandini: Husband's sister

Pitamaha: Grandfather

Pitashree: Father

Pitrushya and *Aatya*: Aunt—father's sister

Pitruvya: Uncle—father's brother

Poutra: Grandson

Swashreyi: Sister's daughter

Swasura: Uncle by marriage—father's sister's husband; also means father-in-law

Swasruva: Mother-in-law

Syala: Wife's brother

Vadhunika: Brother's wife

Vahni: Elder sister

Acknowledgements

Grateful remembrances to Late Shree Ajjarapu Venkata Rao, whose deeply researched work *Krishna Charitra* in Telugu provided valuable inputs for *Ashtamahishi*.

The sources for Shree Vekata Rao's research, as listed by him, included *The Krishnavatara* by the legendary Kanaiyalal Maneklal Munshi (K.M. Munshi); *Andhra Mahabharatam* by 'Kavitrayam'—Nannaya, Thikkana and Yerrapragada; and *Andhra Maha Bhagavatamu* by Bammera Potana, popularly known as *Potana Bhagavatam*.

Krishna Charitra, a monumental work running into more than 5,000 pages, was published in February 2018.

My grateful thanks to Smt. P. Shanta Devi, for generously sharing the manuscript of her father's work with me.